GOLDEN ARMOUR

THE SPURS

Also available in this series:

And coming soon:

THE SPURS

Richard Brown

SCHOLASTIC

Scholastic Children's Books,
Commonwealth House, 1–19 New Oxford Street,
London WC1A 1NU, UK
a division of Scholastic Ltd
London ~ New York ~ Toronto ~ Sydney ~ Auckland
Mexico City ~ New Delhi ~ Hong Kong

First published in the UK by Scholastic Ltd, 2000

ISBN 0 439 01207 4

Typeset by DP Photosetting, Aylesbury, Bucks
Printed by The Bath Press, Bath

2 4 6 8 10 9 7 5 3 1

THE ORIGIN OF THE GOLDEN ARMOUR

In the midst of a treacherous sea, there is a tiny island. It is temperate and beautiful all the year round. But no one lives there, for it is bewitched. At the heart of it is a ruined temple – and a broken paradise.

It is all that is left of a vast island which Citatha, the goddess of nature, once reigned over. The climate was sunny and calm, and nature was always in balance. The temple at the centre of the island was magnificent then. Statues and pictures of the goddess were everywhere in shrines and alcoves, groves and gardens. She wore flowers in her hair, a robe made of lilies and a cloak sewn with a hundred different leaves. Graceful, silver-haired cats slipped in and out of the temple columns, like the spirits of past priestesses.

And then, catastrophe! A huge volcano spewed up masses of ash and lava. Its force was so great, it split the island into four. Tidal-waves poured over the land and vast tracts of Citatha's world fell into the boiling sea.

When the air cleared, she saw there was nothing left but four distant islands, shrouded in ash and full of death. Only a fragment of her paradise remained, and in the ruins of her deserted temple she grieved for her lost world.

In time, North Island became cold and bleak, East Island a burning desert, West Island a land of fogs, and on South Island the rain made the land perpetually flooded.

In sorrow, Citatha dreamed a great dream. Out of her dream there stepped a suit of golden armour, etched with many glittering patterns.

Citatha entered the Golden Armour and infused it with her magic. She imbued it with nature. Then she left it to do its destined work.

It rested in the deepest vault of the ruined temple. The Helmet shimmered with frost. The Shield hummed with a hot and scouring wind. The Spurs were shrouded in mist. And raindrops glittered on the scabbard of the Sword.

For centuries it has waited there in that deep and sacred vault. Parts of it have by mysterious means found their way to the islands. There, hidden by time, they await the coming of those who can release the magic within them.

Only then will Citatha's reign be restored. And only then will the four islands become like the paradise they once were, beautiful and calm.

CHAPTER 1

Lord Tancred's ship manoeuvred mysteriously through the jagged rocks that lurked in the grey and choppy seas. He and his captain had no need to consult their maps: they accepted that the ship was guided by the unseen hand of the goddess Citatha, on whose mission they were bound.

Tancred's children, twelve-year-old twins Cassie and Keiron, were leaning on a balustrade on the upper deck, sea salt in their long, bleached hair. The first days at sea had been warm, calm and restful and they had enjoyed it; but now the wind had picked up and it was growing colder.

"We're about halfway, then," said Cassie.

"I should think West Island's a bit nearer than that."

"No," she said, smiling. "I meant…" She looked into her brother's wide brown eyes. "Two of Citatha's islands are like the paradise they used to be, before the Catastrophe. Now it's West Island – and the Spurs."

"Ah, the Spurs. I wonder what sort of magic they will have?"

Cassie shrugged. "What danger they will put us in, you mean. So many things could have gone wrong – *did* go wrong – on the other islands. Why not this one?"

They were talking about the Golden Armour. Its Helmet, Shield, Spurs and Sword had long ago been taken by unknown hands and had become scattered mysteriously throughout the four islands. The twins and their father, in the teeth of the most extraordinary adventures, had restored the Helmet and the Shield to the Armour. Now, at Citatha's bidding they were sailing to West Island to find the Golden Spurs.

Keiron asked his little wooden manikin, Will, *What do you think lies ahead?* He had carved Will, who was no bigger than his hand, out of a piece of willow back on North Island, and his sister, with her innate gift for life-giving, had brought him alive. Keiron alone could speak to him, and that only telepathically.

Will sometimes experienced prophetic flashes; but this time he said, *It's puzzling. All I see is a swirling fog, with a sort of diamond at the centre. I don't see spurs.*

Their father, his white beard and hair whipped by the wind, climbed the steps to the upper deck. "We're not far off the coast now." He took a map from his pocket and unrolled it. "We should land in the south-east. See," he said, pointing to a harbour. "Here. This part of the island is inhabited: there are what look like eleven big country estates on three sides of the city. And there's only one city. The rest of the island is a forest, vast tracts of it where few people live."

Cassie pointed to an island on a lake just above the city. "That looks pretty," she said. "I wonder whether anyone lives there?" She looked closer and saw a tiny

4

sketch of what in real life was a great sprawling building. It was one which she would grow to hate.

"And what's that?" Keiron asked, pointing to a tall tower perched on the north-eastern coast. A black flying horse had been drawn on its pinnacle.

"We'll find out in time," said Tancred. The picture of the silhouetted horse and its rider made him uneasy, and he shuddered inwardly: a dim memory of a dark story he had read hovered at the back of his mind.

He pointed to an extinct volcano in the middle of the great forest. "I'm sure I've read legends about that. Something to do with a Mooncastle."

They pored over the map, building fantastic constructions on the sketchiest of information.

But when, later, the island itself hove into sight, they were in for a disappointment. Their telescopes revealed that it was shrouded in a mantle of grey fog. Nothing could be seen but a few ghostly trees and looming rocks in the thick pall.

"I thought the stories about this fog were exaggerated, but I'm not so sure now," Tancred murmured.

"Surely it's not always like this?" Keiron objected.

"What a contrast to East Island!" Cassie observed ironically.

The crew manoeuvred the ship into a natural harbour. As it neared the island, a chill damp mist crept over them. The twins hurried below deck, pulled on coats and stuffed warmer clothes into the packs they had got ready for their stay on the island.

They stood on the lower deck, their packs strapped to their backs. The wall of mist closed over them, striking cold and wet on their faces. Everything became grey and hazy, robbed of its colour, glistening with damp.

"If we can find the Golden Spurs in this..." Keiron began, shivering.

"...and blow away this terrible fog..."

"It'll be a miracle!"

Their father was arguing with the captain of the crew.

He gestured to his children to get into the boat that would take them to the shore. "I'm afraid the crew refuse to come with us. They say the island is full of deadly ghosts. We shall have to go alone. Can you carry your own things?"

The twins nodded. They looked at the grim and apprehensive faces of the crew who were standing about the ship, watching them silently. What had they heard about the place that made it so frightening?

"I'm sorry, Miss," the captain said to Cassie, feeling ashamed of his caution.

"As long as you're here when we come back," said Cassie, trying to make light of it.

"We shall be, Miss, don't worry."

Tancred clambered into the boat after his children and took the oars.

The boat glided to a halt beside the wooden quay and figures emerged out of the mist to help them land. A knot of curious harbour workers formed around them. They were all thin, grey-skinned – or was that merely the effect of the ghostly light? – and the pupils of their eyes were wide and dark.

"Look at their ears," Keiron whispered to Cassie. They were perhaps twice as large as the twins' ears and protruded outward. Cassie noticed that they twitched, like the ears of a cat.

Tancred explained who he was. The fact that he was so distinguished a visitor – when visitors were so rare – caused quite a stir. The ruler of North Island, here!

"If my researches are correct," Tancred was saying, "you do not have just one ruler here."

"We have a Council," one of them said. "It's made up from the chief of each of the Eleven Families. You will have to report to the Council as soon as you arrive in the City."

"Then lead the way."

But no one moved. "We stay here," someone explained. "We are harbour people, we don't go inland."

"But surely one of you…?"

Several shook their heads.

"Oh, well, at least you'll be good enough to point me in the direction of the City?"

They led Tancred and the twins to a shingled, weed-strewn road winding into the forest. "Keep to this and you won't get lost."

"On foot? Don't you have any horses or mules we could hire?"

Again, they shrugged; there was no need for horses or mules here.

Tancred and the twins set off. Within a few minutes the sea, the harbour, the people were swallowed up in the clinging mist.

They strode on in silence. It was good to walk after being confined to a ship. The road was like a dark tunnel through the trees. There was so little to see, just the occasional swirl of mist; and there was no sound, either. It was eerie: at any time someone might spring out on them, or perhaps some hideous creature might leap down on them from the shadowy branches.

Trees don't believe in an underworld, said Will. *But if we did, it would be just like this.*

"Why is it like this?" Keiron wondered.

"On North Island it was always cold and windy," Tancred reminded them. "And on East Island, scorching hot. Well, here they suffer perpetual fog."

"Well, I think this is the worst," Cassie declared. She wiped the moisture from her face. "It's like being half-blind."

"Yes, it's hard to make out what things are," Keiron agreed.

Further on, two rocks loomed up in the mist. At first, they thought they were men, and Tancred, pausing several yards away, hailed them. They found their mistake disturbing rather than funny.

A crashing sound in the wood set their hearts beating fast. They crouched at the foot of a tree and waited to see what would emerge. A large creature, slim as a horse but with extraordinary horns, clattered on to the shingle road and paused in front of them, sniffing the air, its pale yellow eyes wide and glowing. Taking fright, it jerked away from them and galloped down the road.

"The forest is not entirely lifeless, then," Tancred observed with satisfaction. He reached into a tree. "Look at the leaves," he said, fingering one. "They're tough. They'd have to be to survive in this appalling light."

They're hardly trees as I know them, said Will. *More like ghost-trees.*

"Do you think there are other creatures in the forest?" Cassie asked, peering into the swirling fog. They listened, as if that might give her an answer, but all they could hear was the condensed mist dripping off the leaves.

In the late afternoon, the pallid light began to fade. Tancred was getting worried: he did not want his children to have to spend a night in this damp and creepy place. But as the shadows deepened, he suggested that they make camp.

Not here, said Will. *Just a bit further.*

Why? What's wrong with here?

I don't know. Just a feeling.

"Will says, go a bit further," said Keiron, striding ahead.

Cassie sighed; she was getting tired.

"Look, there's a clearing," Keiron shouted. But it was more a crossroads. To their delight, there was a road sign carved in wood. It said, *The Estate of the Storyteller*, and it pointed down a narrow track at right angles to the main one.

"A strange name for a place," said Tancred. "But where there's an estate, there's civilization. Come on, you two, you might get a bed for the night after all."

An hour later they pushed open a gate set in a great wall. Inside, a ragged path led them through the estate grounds to a large, elegant house that was full of flickering lights. A flight of stone steps led up to glass double doors. Much of the building seemed to be made of thick glass, perhaps to make the best of the restricted light. Tancred pulled on the bell-pull and they listened to a bell booming deep in the bowels of the house.

An old servant answered the door. A flicker of surprise crossed his otherwise lined and impassive face. He showed them into a cavernous lobby full of tall paintings, and asked them to wait.

"Look at this," said Keiron. Set like a mosaic in the floor was a picture of two spurs side by side, like mirror images of themselves.

"And this," said Cassie, pointing to a large pair of ornamental spurs hanging above a fireplace.

"It's a pity they're not gold," Tancred observed dryly. "Our mission might have been over almost before it had begun!"

A small, energetic man in a long green robe swept in.

"Welcome, indeed," he said, extending his hands. His grey eyes were sparkling with curiosity. "I am Councillor Torke."

As Tancred told him who they were, Torke's sharp, darting eyes grew wide, his words tumbled out excitedly, and his hands gesticulated. He was "honoured beyond measure" to have so distinguished a foreigner, and "enchanted" to play host to "these beautiful, beautiful twins".

"I can't be with you right now," he said apologetically. "But we will be able to talk in the morning. When you have eaten, you must join us in the ballroom. We are in the middle of a storytelling session – we hold them weekly and everyone comes in from the estate to listen and join in."

He shook Tancred's hand vigorously again, ruffled the twins' hair with both hands, let out a sort of wild shriek, and scampered off. The twins laughed the minute he had gone; he was quite an antidote to the gloom of the place.

After they had cleaned up and eaten a hasty meal, the old servant showed them into the ballroom.

Ah, now this is better, said Will. *Like a campfire in the wood.*

Fires blazed in huge grates either side of the room. There was a large chair against the wall opposite the main entrance, on which sat Councillor Torke. Members of his family sat on chairs either side of him. Around them were perhaps nearly a hundred servants and Estate workers. They were all listening raptly to the Councillor, who broke off his story at Tancred's entry. Everyone turned to look, and there was much whispering.

"Come in, come in, my distinguished friends," Torke shouted, jumping up and beckoning with both his arms. "I've told them who you are and where you have come from. We are all agog to hear your story."

Chairs were vacated beside Torke's chair and the three were seated, facing the eager and expectant audience.

"We always welcome new stories," said a woman wearing a long beige gown. They soon discovered she was Torke's partner, Marsia, one of the best storytellers in the room. "Any visitors – and there are not many – who make their way here, earn the hospitality we lavish on them with their stories."

"If you are sufficiently recovered from your journey," said Torke, with an encouraging smile, "we would hear yours."

Tancred whispered to the twins, "It is their custom. I think we will have to join in."

Torke ushered him to the storytelling chair. Tancred surveyed the sea of expectant faces, lit only by the flames of the fire and candlelight. "Do you know the story of the Golden Armour?" he began, his voice sounding uncertain and thin in the great room. A murmur ran through the audience.

"We know how the goddess Citatha made it, and why," said Marsia. "But we would be happy to hear it again. Every storyteller tells it in a different way."

Tancred had told his children many stories about the islands, their history and mythology, and he had a good memory for them; but he had never had to tell the stories quite like this. Nevertheless, he sat up, cleared his throat, and began. His description of the Great Volcano was so vivid everyone leaned forward in order not to miss a word; and the words he used to describe the making of the armour were so evocative, the audience saw it hovering before their eyes.

"But how did the Spurs find their way here?" Councillor Torke asked, taking his place on the story-telling chair again. It was a favourite question in this storytelling circle, and the twins spent the next hour listening intently to many different versions of the answer. People took their place on the storytelling chair, and the manner of their telling displayed skill and emotion.

Refreshments came round, consisting of wild fruit juice and small, rather bitter cakes, and there was a pause in the storytelling.

Marsia held up her hand for silence. "If Jessie were here, he would tell us a story about his moonhorse, wouldn't he," she smiled. The audience knew that, after a month apart, she was impatient to see her son again. She turned to the twins. "From what your father has said, you must have stories to tell too. Would you honour us?"

Caught unawares, Cassie blushed and Keiron giggled in embarrassment; but, seeing the look on their father's face, they quickly composed themselves. "What shall we tell?" Cassie whispered urgently to her father.

"Tell them what happened to us on North Island. About the Helmet, and Prince Badrur, about the monsters, and the hideous Child."

"I don't think I can," Cassie said, drawing back.

"We'll tell it together," said Keiron. "I'll start, if you like."

He started well, and Cassie, despite her nerves, soon joined in. Will acted like a prompt for Keiron, and Tancred added his own point of view. Never had that seasoned audience been so enthralled.

A huge clock chimed midnight, and the storytelling came to a sudden end. The crowd poured out on to the wide steps above garden and stood about silently, staring at the sky.

"You came on the best night of the month," Torke said to Tancred.

They stood in the damp, chill garden. Only the occasional cough, and the drip, drip of the leaves could be heard. "You're about to see something special," said Marsia to the twins.

And then the fog began to thin. It grew lighter and wispier.

"Look!" shouted someone. "There it is!"

People pointed into the sky. Suddenly, a full, round, bright silver moon broke free of the swirling, thinning fog. Everyone cheered. The light transformed the garden; the people broke into smiles and happy chatter; the fog cleared as if someone was wiping it away with a huge, invisible brush, and a few brave stars glittered in the dark blue.

"For one night," Marsia explained, "every twenty-four days, which marks the cycle of the moon, the fog clears. It is always magical for us. And tomorrow there will be sunshine. It's the only day in the whole month we see sunlight. Tonight, we are happy."

"But why only once a month?" Keiron asked.

"It's a long story," said Torke. "Ask our son Jessie to tell you tomorrow."

"Why isn't he here?" Cassie asked. She sensed how eager both parents were to see him. But no one answered her.

The twins were late getting to bed, and overtired. The beds, in their downstairs bedroom, were vast, damp and lumpy. The candles burnt low before the children finally drifted off to sleep.

Cassie woke with a start. Where was she? For a few seconds she panicked; then she remembered. Bright moonlight was streaming through the tall windows. She sat up and listened; there was no sound, but she felt sure there was a presence outside. She stood by the window. The moon was brightly luminescent, like a great jewel; the shadows on its surface suggested huge lakes. Everthing was bathed in its ghostly light, and Cassie felt she was part of a dream.

Out of the sky, over the dark forest, came a flying moonhorse. White, and silvered by the moon, its huge wings flapped up and down. It was being ridden by a boy about her own age. The moonhorse hovered over the garden and then lowered itself gently on to the grass. The boy patted the horse's neck and then slid off her back. He ran towards the house, whistling loudly to signal his arrival.

The moonhorse folded its wings and nibbled the grass. Cassie thought she had never seen anything so beautiful. She turned the handle on the window and it opened. Stepping out, the stone steps and grass were cold and wet on her bare feet. The moonhorse looked up and watched her, its body alert, ready to canter away.

Cassie stopped a few feet away from it. She saw that in the centre of its forehead was a large, glowing stone, pale and milky as a moonstone. It was not hanging like a tear-drop brooch, it was set into the horse's coat, part of its anatomy. She stepped into the stone's soft light, and felt the moonhorse relax. It looked at her trustingly with large silver-grey eyes.

"Hello," Cassie whispered. "Aren't you beautiful." Tentatively, she reached up and touched the moonhorse's nose. For Cassie, touching the moonhorse was natural; for the creature, it was a sign of extraordinary acceptance. The moonhorse neighed softly, allowing itself to be nuzzled. Cassie shivered, not so much from the cold, as from a sense that she had come in contact with something utterly magical.

"Hey," came a voice across the grass. "Who are you?"

She turned and saw the boy leaning out of an upstairs window. "I'm Cassie," she answered, advancing towards the house.

"Well, Cassie," said the boy. "You're no ordinary girl, are you."

She was now directly below him. He had ginger hair and bright, eager eyes. She thought he was about her own age. "Who are you?" she asked.

"I am Jessie, son of the Councillor."

"Are you the one that flew on the horse?"

"Yes. Did you see me?"

She nodded.

"It's supposed to be a secret."

"I'm sorry. I looked out of the window and..."

"Don't apologize. I think you were meant to see us."

"What do you mean?"

"My moonhorse let you touch her. She would only do that if you were special."

"Oh, there's nothing special about me," Cassie laughed, a little embarrassed.

He glanced back into the room. "Look, it's very late and my mother's calling me," he said. "I'll see you in the morning. You will be here, won't you? It's very important that I talk to you."

She nodded.

"Goodnight, Cassie. I can't wait for the morning." He disappeared and the window closed.

Keiron was sitting up in bed. He saw the starry look in his sister's eyes. "What happened?" She told him, but she could not convey to him the wonderful feeling the moonhorse had given her when she touched it.

They woke to brilliant sunlight. The garden was stirring, its tired leaves and tight buds opening up.

After breakfast, the twins met Jessie in the garden. His skin was greyish, his ears were big, but the pupils of his eyes were smaller now in the sunlight, and they were full of curiosity. "Doesn't it feel good!" he exclaimed, gesturing towards the sunlight. "We only see it every twenty-four days."

As they walked across the pale grass, he studied the twins with undisguised interest. The size of their ears, the colour of their skin, the way the sun had bleached their untidy hair, betrayed their foreignness; but he was more interested in their similarities: their looks, their size, their gestures, all of which said, these are twins. And Jessie had a special interest in that fact.

"Where is your flying horse?" Keiron asked. He was eager to see it.

"She is shy," Jessie answered. "She'll be somewhere on the estate. We'll find her later. Come on, I've got a den of my own. Let's go there." It turned out to be a disused summerhouse. Jessie had made it snug with some old bits of furniture, books and cushions.

When they had settled, Jessie asked, "Tell me why you have come here?"

"To find the Golden Spurs," said Cassie. "You know what we mean?"

He nodded vigorously. "Why?" he asked.

They told him about their mission to make the Golden Armour complete. They told him how they found the Helmet on North Island, and the Shield on East Island, and how they had been able to release the magic of each to transform the islands into something like a paradise. Now the goddess Citatha had sent them to find the Golden Spurs, to release their magic and transform this island too.

"We shall get rid of all this fog," said Keiron, "not just for one day in a month, but for ever."

Jessie was so excited by what he had heard, he wriggled about on his cushion and made strange, high-pitched noises. "If only... If only..." he said, his face bright with hope. "But half your search is already over. I can tell you right now where one of the Golden Spurs is."

"You can?" the twins exclaimed.

"Yes, there's no mystery. It's in a building in the centre of the city, called the Sanctuary of the Spur. It's always been there. We sort of worship it as a symbol of this island. There are spurs everywhere here, you know. You must have seen them in the house."

"So we can't get hold of this Golden Spur?" said Keiron.

"Hold of it?" Jessie laughed, incredulously. "If you tried, you'd be slung in prison. It's very well guarded."

"And the other Spur?" Cassie asked, glancing despondently at her brother.

Jessie shook his head. "No one knows where that is. If we could find it..."

"Yes?"

"Well, everyone believes that if the two Spurs were brought together, the island would be rid of the fog."

"Do you believe that?"

"Yes, I do! But there are many things that have to be in place before it can happen. There are legends..."

"There are always legends," Keiron laughed.

They talked for a while about the island and its legends. Then Jessie said, "I must warn you that if you stay on this island, you will have to go to the school."

"School?" the twins echoed. They had never been to a school themselves.

"There's one great school on the island. It's in the middle of a lake. All the children from the ages of seven to fourteen have to go there. Even the children of Councillors like me."

"What's it like?"

"It's a terrible place. The building's so dark and gloomy."

"Then why don't you stay here?"

"I can't. I wish I could! But by nightfall I will have to return on my moonhorse. We're only let out once a month, on the day the fog clears."

"Can't you escape on your moonhorse?"

"No, she lives here on our Estate. She would only come on Fogclear Night, or if I was in real trouble – she can sense such things."

"And your parents let this happen?" Cassie was indignant.

"They have no choice. It's the law. They went to the same school when they were young, and their parents before them. Besides, from what they've told me, it was much better in their day. They didn't have Mr Groak for a headmaster or Miss Rictus for a teacher. I try to tell them what those two are like, but they just think I'm exaggerating. Anyway, if I tried to run away, it would bring great shame on my family; I can't do that. No, I have no choice."

"I'm sorry," said Cassie. "It sounds dreadful."

"Oh, well, there's one good thing. I see all my friends there. We're all in the same class, all the twelve-year-olds, and we share dormitories. It's great. You'd like them all. And they'd like you."

"Well, our father would never agree to us going to such a school!" Keiron interrupted.

"He wouldn't have a choice," Jessie replied. "He'd be powerless to stop it. If you're so used to your own freedom, if you can't bear to be locked up and be ordered about, you ought to leave now. That school is like a prison. But I hope you won't. You ought to come."

He's right, said Will unexpectedly. *You have to go there whether you like it or not. It's like a seed being blown on the wind: where it lands, there must it grow.*

The moonhorse was standing beside a dark pool, her wings folded, her reflection undulating on the surface of the water. She tossed her head when Keiron approached her; and even in the sunlight he felt the strength of the light cast over him from the moonstone. Her wings ruffled a little in the breeze, and she struck a hoof in the grass. When she lowered her head, Keiron stepped forward and ran a hand down her silvery-white muzzle. A sense of peace, a feeling of attachment and the *rightness* of it, flowed into him. He pressed his face against her warm flank and whispered things to her which the other two, watching intently nearby, could not hear.

"Yes!" Jessie exclaimed to himself.

"What?"

"She's allowed him to touch her too. That's good. That's essential!"

"Can't anyone touch her?"

Jessie shook his head.

When dusk fell, and the moon appeared above the band of dark trees, Jessie had to leave. "It's been a wonderful, fantastic day," he said to the twins. "I hope we meet again."

"So do we," said Keiron with feeling.

Jessie hugged his parents and leapt on to his moonhorse. She rose into the darkening sky, her great flapping wings catching the moonlight; she grew smaller and smaller in the gathering gloom. The twins had taken such a liking to the thin, wiry boy with his bright ginger hair and nervous, high-pitched laugh, they had lumps in their throats as they waved goodbye.

Don't worry, said Will, *you'll see him again. It's where you'll see him you won't like.*

What are you talking about, Will?

Oh, nothing. There was no point in frightening the boy.

The following morning, the fog had descended again. It hung ghostly in the trees and dripped from the eaves of the house.

"We must go to the city," Tancred said, coming into his children's room. "That is the advice Torke and Marsia give. They have given us the use of their town house, so we should be safe."

"Safe?" Cassie echoed.

21

"We are in the dark here," he said, peering out at the blanket of fog. "But at least we only have to find one Spur. That must count as a good start."

Torke and Marsia came down to the gates to see them off. They mounted docile horses which had large eyes and tall pointed ears. "The horses know exactly where to take you," said Torke. "And Damian here –" he pointed to a small, silent man who was standing beside the horse – "will be your guide. He has a letter from me explaining who you are: you should have no trouble getting into the city."

He turned to Tancred. "I supect we have many more stories to share, my lord. You tell them like an expert. There's a fire in your eyes when you speak. We shall meet again soon."

Marsia said to the twins, "I have something for you both." She unwrapped a little blue cloth and took from it two golden chains, on each of which hung an ornamental spur. "These have been in our family for generations. They were given to Jessie at his birth. He won't tell me why, but he insists on you having them while you're here, and he's too shy to give you them himself. He must think very highly of you." She smiled mysteriously. "Put them around your necks. They will give you protection."

The twins were touched and delighted by the gifts. They did not like to ask what the pendant spurs might protect them against. "If only these were the real spurs," Keiron whispered to his sister. "Just think!"

They travelled at an even, monotonous pace through the fog all day, resting occasionally to eat and stretch their legs. Sometimes they heard the distant crashing of some large animal in the woods, or the flapping of a giant bird; otherwise, the silence was broken only by the incessant dripping of the leaves. They got thoroughly soaked, for the damp fog seeped into everything.

The night was miserable for Tancred, who could not sleep; but mercifully, the twins were so tired they slept through the worst of it. The guide, Damian, kept aloof, silent and morose; Tancred wondered whether he had orders not to speak. Will kept Tancred company, and although they could not converse, they drew comfort from each other's presence.

Late the following day, they were suddenly hailed by voices and shadowy figures in the fog ahead. "Who goes there?"

"Guests of Councillor Torke," Tancred shouted back.

They were surrounded by city gatekeepers. It was their job to note who entered and left the city and to report this to the authorities. They were suspicious of the strangers, and might have marched them away to be questioned; but Damian produced Torke's letter, and after it was read they were let through.

Their guide led them through the city towards Torke and Marsia's town house. The fog was a little less dense here: they could see either side of the street and a few yards ahead. The few townspeople who were out and about habitually ran their fingers along grooves in the walls of the buildings: Damian, in a few terse words, explained that these grooves contained a simple code to tell them which street they were in. Lamps glowed in the grey stone houses, revealing people playing musical instruments, or huddled together telling stories, or weaving. In some buildings there were workshops for the making of clothes and pottery and such like.

It was the eerie silence of the place which struck the twins first. The occasional sounds – the banging of a door, a subdued shout, the clop of the horses' hooves on the rough cobbles – were muted by the fog: it was incredibly quiet.

But, as they peered into windows and watched people hurrying by, the twins noticed something else too: there were no children of their own age. Young ones, yes, up to the age of seven, and older ones, almost adult, but no children.

They've transplanted all the saplings, said Will, *to stop them growing wild.*

Well, they won't transplant me! Keiron retorted.

Torke and Marsia's town house was very tall and narrow, five storeys high, sandwiched between two equally tall, slightly rickety houses made of glistening grey slate and stone. All the houses were tall and thin, as if struggling upwards in the gloom, like plants deprived of light.

An old housekeeper showed them around. She mumbled to herself all the time and kept her eyes lowered, as if she did not want to know who they were; but later she appeared and announced that a meal was ready for them. She placed a large stewing pot in the middle of the table, from which issued the most tantalizing smells, and they fell to it thankfully.

They were about to go to bed when there was a loud thumping on the door. A smart young man in a grey military uniform was on the doorstep, flourishing an official-looking letter.

"You are commanded to appear before the Council tomorrow morning at eleven," he said, handing Tancred the letter. "Do not fail this summons."

His gaze fell on the twins who were hovering behind their father. "Get them ready for the school," he added, almost as an aside.

Tancred closed the door.

"Father," Keiron said, turning on him, even as Tancred was breaking the seal of the letter. "You must not let them send us to this school. Jessie told us about it. It sounds hideous."

Tancred scanned the letter, then looked at his children anxiously. "This says that I must put myself at the disposal of the Ruling Council, and you must attend the school. It is they who make the laws."

The twins looked at each other in dismay. To be separated from their father and be forced to go to a prison-like school – the prospect made them speechless.

"Don't worry," said Tancred. "I spoke to Marsia about it. It's not half as bad as Jessie makes out, I'm sure. You'll make good friends there. And besides, what better place to find out all there is to know about this island? Keep that in mind."

But the twins stared at him unconvinced, and their hearts sank.

CHAPTER 2

Before breakfast, the twins explored the house. In every room they found a spur: it might be a real one, or a picture of one, or even a sculpted one. "They certainly believe in the power of the Spurs to protect them," said Keiron.

"But against what?" Cassie wondered, peering out into the shrouded street. A few people were hurrying past, most of them wearing long, grey, hooded gowns, their faces hidden. "Jessie didn't say there were any monsters here, did he?"

It's more in their imagination, said Will.

What do you mean?

I don't know. Like ghosts. Are they real or not?

If you're just going to talk in riddles…

"What's he saying?" said Cassie. She could tell when her brother was talking telepathically to Will by the slight, attentive tip of his head and a brief, inward look in his eyes.

"Oh, nothing. Something about ghosts."

"Well, this is a ghostly place."

"Come on, I'm hungry. I wonder if that creepy old housekeeper's got something for us to eat."

They found a large, warm loaf of bread on the table, some preserves, milk, butter and fruit; the milk proved sour, and the fruit hard and bitter, but the twins tucked in gratefully without waiting for their father.

"I don't want to go to this school," said Keiron. He'd had vague nightmares about it, and the horror of them still lingered in his mind.

"Nor the Council," said Cassie. "Perhaps we can escape somewhere. Go back to the storyteller's Estate. It was nice there."

"There's no escape," came the lugubrious voice of the housekeeper. She was standing in the shadowy doorway, arms folded. "We all do as we are told here. No one goes against the law."

Her presence killed any desire to talk.

Suddenly, she began to cough. It was not an ordinary irritation of the throat, it welled up from sickly lungs and wracked her whole body. The twins, alarmed, jumped up to try and help, but she shooed them away. "I'm sorry," she said weakly, shuffling into the passage. They heard her cough fade into the house.

"The poor thing," Cassie said. "I could have helped her if she'd have let me."

"She wouldn't have, though. Best keep your healing powers to yourself for now, until we find out what's going on here."

"It's the damp. It's bound to give people the cough here. She sounded really ill, though, didn't she."

The housekeeper, having recovered from her fit of coughing, gave them directions to the Council Chamber. They set off on foot.

The fog hung pallid and wet. People emerged from it and were sucked back into it like drifting phantoms. A few young children were playing in a courtyard, and followed them curiously for a while; but when the twins paused to talk to them, they ran away, shrieking with exaggerated fear.

The winding, narrow streets soon gave way to a square which, even in the fog, seemed huge. As they walked across it, they could just make out life-size stone carvings of winged horses set at the four corners. A great mosaic depicting two giant spurs was set in a circle at the square's centre. There was a short flight of steps to an impressive looking building with many tall, arched windows. Surmounting the building was a giant metal spur, its wheel turning slowly in the breeze, creaking in the silence.

Several soldiers in grey uniforms appeared out of the fog and demanded to know their business. Silently, Tancred handed them the letter. They scanned it, looked at them with renewed interest, and then two of them escorted Tancred and the twins up the steps and into the building. Lamps burnt everywhere. They were shown into a long narrow room with benches against the walls, and told to wait until the Council was ready to talk to them. There they had to kick their heels for most of the day. Tancred twice reminded the officer who seemed to be in charge who he was, but it had no effect.

The room gradually filled up with people – "petitioners" the officer called them – but when the twins tried to engage them in conversation, they shook their heads or shooed them away or looked embarrassed, as if talking was not their custom in such a place.

Mid-afternoon, Tancred's patience snapped. "We're leaving," he said, his eyes hot with anger. He marched with the twins towards the main entrance, but before they could get out they were surrounded by uniformed officers and firmly ordered to return to the waiting-room. Tancred protested loudly, and the twins were getting frightened that he might overdo it – for, though he was on the surface a placid, thoughtful man, passions ran deep in him, and these could flare up under provocation – when his name was called by a Council usher. It was time at last for them to enter the Council Chamber.

They stepped into a huge room. Tall windows suffused the vast space with a sort of pearly light, augmented by a row of lamps around the perimeter. In the centre of the chamber, on a raised platform, was a giant, half-moon table at which sat, on high chairs, the eleven Councillors, resplendent in ceremonial robes. Below them was a smaller table where three officials sat, with pens poised above great ledgers. Other officials sat in the shadows, as silent witnesses; and facing the Councillors was a dais with a rail where the petitioners had to stand to address the Chamber.

Tancred was ushered to this dais while the twins were held back. He scanned the faces of the Councillors. They were all middle-aged or older, some women, some men. He recognized Torke, who must have arrived that morning, and was about to greet him, but Torke ever so faintly shook his head, and Tancred, understanding, held his tongue.

"My Lord Tancred, forgive us for the delay. We have had many petitioners today, whom the law says we must deal with before any other matters. As a ruler yourself, we feel sure you will understand."

There were a lot of polite formalities that seemed to the twins to go on for ever. Tancred explained his purpose in coming to the island, and there was much talk of the goddess Citatha and the Golden Armour. He was persuaded to tell the Council what had happened on North Island and on East Island – for Torke had told them that the Golden Helmet and the Shield had been found – and for an hour he relived all the high points of their quest for the Helmet and the Shield, of their conflict with Prince Badrur and the monsters, of the battle between the scorpion-guards and lizard-people, and of the magical transformation of the islands. He told it so well, there was applause from the Councillors when he had finished.

"Well, my lord," said one of the Councillors, a tall woman with raven-black hair, "we have been vastly entertained – and I may say, disturbed a little too – by what you have told us. Councillor Torke here should look out, we might well have found a rival storyteller on the island." There was a polite chuckling at her joke, and Torke grimaced good-humouredly. "Now, we must decide what to do with you while you are here."

"To do with me?" Tancred said, challengingly.

She glanced at the others, as if this had already been discussed among them. "Yes, if you are to stay, you must be employed usefully, and be where we can keep an eye on you."

"I rather protest at that. I am used to my own freedom."

"Of course, as a lord, you would be," another Councillor interjected acidly.

The raven-haired Councillor flashed her colleague a warning glance and said in explanation, "You see, Lord Tancred, we may all have inherited our position on this Council, but we are still democratic here. We each represent a portion of the city and look after our people's needs. We understand that you were in sole charge on North Island?"

"Perhaps so, yes, but..."

"Then you're rather like the Queen of East Island. We do not believe in monarchs and dictators here. In fact, we abhor them. If you had been her, a ruler who, you have told us, used to terrorize her people with monsters in the shape of scorpions, you would have been deported straight away. But you appear to be a mixture of her and us. That rather intrigues us, and we wish to know more! So, what we have in mind for you is this. You will visit each of the Eleven Estates of the Hereditary Councillors and be our honoured guest in each. You will tell us about North Island; you will tell us the mythology of it; and you will tell us all you know as a result of your recent adventures on East Island, too. You will become an itinerant storyteller, which we think best befits your obvious talents."

Tancred was about to protest again; but then he realized that this would give him wide access to all the people in power, their Estates and city houses – just what he needed to help him find the missing Golden Spur. So he bowed and smiled and said how honoured he was.

"As for your children..." said the raven-haired Councillor.

Tancred saw the look of appeal in his children's eyes. "They will come with me, of course," he butted in smoothly.

There was a murmur of protest from several Councillors. The raven-haired one shook her head. "It is against our strict laws to have children of that age roaming the island. It would set a precedent which would be too awkward for us. No, their place is in the school with the other children of the city."

The twins had been silent long enough, and this was their cue.

"No," Keiron shouted. "We don't want to."

"We shan't go," Cassie protested at the same time. "Father, tell them!"

"Silence," the raven-haired Councillor thundered, her dark eyes glittering. "Here, the children obey their parents."

Tancred argued heatedly for his children, but the Council were deaf to his pleas. He turned to the twins with a look of despair. "I would leave now if I could," he said. "But you know we cannot leave until..."

He turned and as a last resort pleaded with Torke.

"It's the best we can do," Torke said, shaking his head apologetically. "Remember, all of us here on this Council have a child at the school – all, as it happens, the same age as your children. They will be in good company." He turned to the twins. "You will see Jessie there. You will be in his class. You will make friends with our children, and we shall all like that. It won't be so bad as you think."

"But we've always been with our father," Cassie said.

"He's always taught us," Keiron added.

"You'll be able to see him on Fogless Day each month, like the other children," the raven-haired Councillor said. "Now, Lord Tancred, if you have any last words for your children, you should say them now. They are setting off for the school immediately."

That shocked Tancred: he thought they would be given a few days together before being parted. "This is outrageous," he fumed, but no amount of protest moved the Councillors. They sat back and watched Tancred impassively as he turned to his children with tears of rage, of sadness, in his eyes.

Tancred stood on the foggy, twilight bank of the vast, metal-grey lake to the north of the city, and watched as the twins were rowed out over the glassy surface, towards a great shadowy smudge of a building on the water's horizon. He waved despondently until they faded into the gauzy grey curtain that hung everywhere in this dismal place. "I shall do my best to get you out of that place as soon as I can," he had promised them; but as he turned and saw the three guards keeping a watch on him a little way off, he knew that that would not be easy.

The twins had locked arms in the boat and watched as the school loomed out of the fog like a great black cloud creeping over the sky. They felt wretched and angry. How dare these people treat them like this! And then, to see the look of despair on their father's face.

Couldn't you have foreseen this? Keiron asked Will bitterly. What was the use of a manikin that caught glimpses of the future if he didn't give warnings?

Sometimes we're all just leaves in the wind, Will answered dejectedly.

That's not much help.

I know; but if I could foresee everything that was going to happen to you here, you'd never have come. Besides, something tells me you have to come here to find the missing Spur. So try and look on the bright side.

The two men who were ferrying them across the lake dipped their oars rhythmically, and the boat moved swiftly towards a rock jetty.

They picked their way apprehensively along the slippery jetty, which ended in a tall, bolt-studded door in the dark, towering walls of the school. The sound of the knocker echoed deep inside the cavernous building, and the wait for someone to answer seemed interminably long. Cassie shivered and looked back at the inky water. Perhaps they could jump in that and swim away to safety? Keiron, sensing her desperate thought, squeezed her hand. He was annoyed that his heart was beating apprehensively: he was determined that whatever they were to encounter in this hideous place, he would acquit himself with dignity and bravery. There was no turning back now.

The door creaked open, and in the light from a lamp held aloft the twins saw a tall, bony woman in a long black gown. Her thin hair, scragged up at the back, was grey, but her eyebrows, which tufted out in all directions, were like great black smudges on a dead white face. She lowered the lamp towards the twins, so that her face was lit luridly from below, turning it into an inflamed and frightening mask, illuminating the red rims around her grey eyes.

The twins recoiled at the sight.

"What have we here?" she said. "Two children that I've never seen before? Impossible! Where have you two been hiding?" The syllables of her words ran together, so that her voice was like a vine, twisting and turning, looking for ways to tighten its grip.

"Visitors from North Island," one of the men explained, and he handed her a letter from the Council. She took it with a long, bony hand, saw the seal and nodded with evident satisfaction. She read the letter slowly. "Now, that is interesting. Come, let me look at you." She held the lamp close to them. "Twins, too. I hope that doesn't mean trouble."

Keiron scowled at that. "We didn't ask to come here," he said.

Her eyes narrowed and her expression became hard.

"We don't want to be here," said Cassie. "It's all a mistake."

"Be quiet, both of you! There are no mistakes here. Wipe out of your mind that you shouldn't be here. This is where you belong." A brief, cruel smile flitted across her bloodless lips. "Step inside."

She slammed the door behind them and the noise boomed down a long, dark corridor.

"I am Miss Rictus," she said, baring her yellow teeth as she enunciated her name. "I will be your form teacher. You will always do as I say. No disobedience is allowed here. Now, follow me , and I will show you to your dormitory."

But Cassie couldn't move. The darkness of the place, the oppressive atmosphere, the wrench from her father, the awfulness of this woman, all combined to paralyse her. She stood there, a look of such distress on her face, Keiron put his arm round her to comfort her. He was feeling much the same.

Miss Rictus glared at them. If there was one thing she couldn't bear, it was giving in to one's feelings. "Come on, you stupid girl," she shouted. She gripped Cassie's wrist and wrenched her forward; her long nails dug into Cassie's flesh, and the girl screamed.

"Leave her alone," Keiron shouted, and he pushed angrily at the woman.

Miss Rictus let go of Cassie and reeled against the wall. For a moment she looked startled. Then her face grew ugly. "You'll regret that, boy. Just because you're the son of some foreign lord, don't think you will be able to get away with behaviour like that. I shall report this to Headmaster Groak. He'll make an example of you, you can be sure of that. Now, move. Or do you want to be shut in the Dark Room on your first night here?"

CHAPTER 3

They climbed flights of dark stairs smelling of damp and age, and came to two doors opposite each other in a passage.

"You, boy, in here," Miss Rictus said, opening the left door. "With the other boys." She lowered her voice. "They've been in bed an hour or so, so don't wake them. There is a bed just inside the door."

It hadn't occurred to the twins that they were to be separated so soon, and they barely had time to glance at each other before Miss Rictus pushed Keiron into the boys' dormitory and closed the door behind him. He felt furious, but he just managed to control himself: there was no point in making more trouble.

He could just make out half a dozen beds in a small room. There were sounds of regular breathing, but as he sat gingerly on his bed, he became aware that other occupants of the room were peering at him in the gloom.

"Jessie," he whispered loudly. "Are you in here?"

A body uncurled from the bed next to his and sat up. "Keiron? Is that really you?"

Keiron breathed a sigh of relief.

The two boys huddled together on Jessie's bed.

"I'm sorry for you," said Jessie. "When you said your father wouldn't let you be sent here, I knew you were wrong, but I couldn't say anything."

"It's a hideous place. I didn't think it was going to be as bad as this."

"You thought I was exaggerating, didn't you." Jessie smiled. "But you get used to the building. It's Mr Groak and Miss Rictus you've got to watch out for." His eyesight was used to the dark, and he could see the scared look on Keiron's face. "Don't worry. I've told the others you and Cassie were coming. They're a bit suspicious of foreigners – we've all grown up together here, you see, so it might not be easy for some of them to accept you straight away."

Cassie was lying fully clothed in her bed, listening to the breathing of the girls in the dormitory. She felt sure some of them were awake and watching her, but no one approached her for some time.

Then, just as she began to relax, a head loomed over her. "We know who you are," said the head.

Cassie looked into bright green eyes and a shock of hair so thick and wild she doubted it had ever been brushed. There was a woody smell about the girl, too, which she found reassuring. "I'm Cassie," she whispered. "Who are you?"

"Astar."

"Hello, Astar," she said uncertainly. She pulled back the bedclothes and sat up.

"That bed's been sitting there empty ever since I can remember," Astar said. "Almost as if it has been waiting for you."

"It's damp," Cassie complained.

Astar grinned. "Everything's damp here. How did you like Miss Rictus?"

Cassie shivered theatrically. "What a dragon!"

There were some giggles from the other beds; it seemed the whole dormitory was listening.

"Keiron – that's my brother – pushed her against the wall. She says we're in trouble." Several girls gasped on hearing that.

Astar saw the glint of the spur on the chain around Cassie's neck. She lifted it for a closer look, then smiled, the hint of suspicion fading from her eyes. "When you're being humiliated tomorrow," she said softly, "think of the spur around your neck. It'll protect you."

Astar melted back into the darkness. Cassie got the impression that she'd have liked to have talked for longer, but was afraid of being caught.

When the dormitory subsided into sleep, Cassie set herself to wait patiently for the first glimmers of dawn through the barred windows, not thinking sleep would come. But she dreamed of riding the moonhorse she had seen at Jessie's, and the soft, rhythmic flap of its great wings through the clouds eventually lulled her into an uneasy sleep.

Keiron was kept awake by one of the boys coughing intermittently through the night, the same sort of deep, tearing cough that the old housekeeper had; he felt sorry for the boy. He must tell Cassie about him, she would soon cure him with her healing hands.

He must have fallen off to sleep, though, for he woke to quite a commotion.

A grey light filled the dormitory.

"Hey, Keiron," Jessie was laughing. "We've been getting acquainted with Will. He's been running over our beds, pulling our ears and jumping in our hair. Look!"

Several boys had gathered around one bed in their crumpled nightgowns, and Will was leaping from one outstretched hand to another. The boys were laughing: never had they seen such a curious and wild little creature.

"He's a real show-off, sometimes," Keiron smiled.

"You'd better keep him hidden from the teachers," Jessie warned. "They like nothing better than confiscating things."

A great gong reverberated through the corridors and into the dormitories. At the signal, the children filed out of many doors and moved silently down the long corridor.

"We're on the third floor," Jessie explained as they shuffled down two flights of wooden stairs. "The second floor is for the workshops. The first is for the classrooms and the hall. And the basement is where we eat; it has the punishment cells, too."

"What are they for?" Cassie asked. She had come up behind her brother and briefly squeezed his arm.

"Oh, they throw us in there to cool us off – when it all gets too much for us."

"Stop talking, there!" the voice of a teacher cried out, and Jessie, stiffening, looked ahead of him, feigning innocence. Cassie looked for the teacher, but all she could see were rows of faces moving impassively ahead, pretending not to see her. Astar nudged her on: it was only a small gesture, but it was noticed.

"Astar, she may be new here, but they teach even foreigners to walk." It was Miss Rictus's sarcastic voice.

Like an automaton, Astar mumbled, "Yes, Miss Rictus."

They all filed into a huge dark dining-room and sat on benches at long, polished tables.

"Just do as we do," Jessie said. "Try and blend in."

Each class sat at their own table. Cassie counted thirteen in her class, all twelve-year-olds; it was the smallest of the classes. There were perhaps five hundred children in the room, she thought, making a swift calculation. She had never seen so many children congregated in one place.

Most of the time the children kept their heads down, as if they were eating alone in the vast hall; but with the rare presence of two newcomers, rumoured to be from another island, many surreptitious glances were cast in the twins' direction, and there was a buzz of curiosity which could be felt if not heard.

They were all served plates of steaming gruel by the oldest children. It was almost inedible without sugar, but when Keiron asked for some, his voice sounding unnaturally loud above the subdued clatter of plates and cutlery, there was a shocked look on the servers' faces. "Sh!" Jessie whispered. "You're not allowed to talk."

Miss Rictus loomed over their table, tapping a spoon in her bony hand and glaring hard at Keiron. The glint in her flinty eyes was enough to silence them all, and for the first time, Keiron felt afraid of her.

* * *

Miss Rictus was seated at her raised desk as they filed into the dusty little classroom where the twelve-year-olds were taught. A pictorial map of the island, its colours faded, hung on the wall one side of her desk, and another map, showing all the islands, hung on the other. Behind her was a blackboard on which had been written:

The Guidance of the Sacred Spur.
This month's precept: Obedience.

Keiron and Cassie slid on to a bench fixed to a disused and dusty desk among several such desks at the back of the room.

"Separate!" Miss Rictus barked at them, and Keiron, scowling, slid over to another one. He resented the way he was talked to here; it made his usually happy nature smoulder.

"The Credo," Miss Rictus said.

The class stood, bowed their heads and mumbled,

"We give allegience to the Spur.
We believe in the Six Precepts.
We shall not deviate, for if we do
The moonghosts will suck out our breath
And devour our lungs. Amen."

Cassie shot a glance at Keiron and shook her head slightly, as if to say, *What is this place we have landed in?*

Keiron felt for Will curled up in his breast pocket, keeping out of sight.

Are you awake, Will?

No, I'm fast asleep. This is your nightmare, not mine. Thanks.

The class sat and stared at Miss Rictus with glazed expressions.

"We have two latecomers to our class – very late! Be warned: their souls are dark and rebellious. They come from wild, barbarian shores." She allowed herself a dry little cackle. "You will all assist myself, and Mr Groak, and the school, to see that they fit in as quickly as possible. Correct their speech, their habits, and above all their ideas, for though they may look innocent, their hearts are seething with sedition. I caught a foul glimpse of that last night. Beware: in the matter of these untutored twins, you are all on trial."

Jessie turned his head slightly to give the faintest of smiles to Keiron. It was no more than a slight movement, but Miss Rictus pounced on it and harangued the boy with such an outpouring of invective, smooth in its delivery yet cutting in its effect – at least upon the twins – that they were astounded. They looked pityingly at Jessie, expecting him at any moment to jump up, shout, rush out in protest; but he sat there with the slightest smirk on his face, as if the words crashing down on his head were no more than leaves blown up by a breeze.

Miss Rictus, temporarily running out of steam, turned to a large model of a spur beside her desk. "May I remind you that when the wheel of the Spur was spun in the Sanctuary at the beginning of the month, *Obedience* was the precept it settled on." She spun the wheel of the spur. On each of its spokes was engraved a moral precept: obedience, humility, faith, fear, vigilance and silence.

"Given that this month our classroom has been invaded by two unruly foreigners, who have so much to learn, this was indeed prescient. Note this, you children of the northern ruler, obedience is the basis of everything here." She wagged her finger at the twins and narrowed her eyes in warning.

Keiron gathered enough courage to say, "Our father is a wise man, and he taught us to think for ourselves."

"It seems he did not teach you obedience," Miss Rictus said acidly.

"He didn't need to," Cassie joined in. "We knew when it was right for us to do what he said."

"There!" thundered Miss Rictus, slapping her hand down on the table. "Note that example of their barbarity. *Deciding for themselves what is right.* It is outrageous! We all have a great challenge here, class."

The twins glanced at each other in disgust and despair. The rest of the class sat motionless, their backs straight, their hands folded neatly on their desks, their eyes staring straight ahead.

Miss Rictus fished a large grey rag from her black gown and wiped her sharp nose. Then she turned to a thin girl with greying hair and thick glasses. "I believe they call you Wag when they think I'm not listening?" she said with a pitying smile.

The girl blushed and did not know where to look.

"Well? It's a simple question."

"Yes, Miss Rictus."

"And why do they call you such a juvenile name?"

Wag stared at the desk. "Because I'm the daughter of my father's Estate."

"For the benefit of our foreigners, explain what that means."

Wag said, "Each of the Eleven Estates has an Ancient Theme. Mine is Law and Order."

"And therefore you wag your fingers at those who transgress," Miss Rictus added, with a peculiar little titter. Composing herself, she added, "Tell us what happens to those who persistently rebel. Who are not susceptible to punishment or reason."

Wag glanced down in distress. Although the rest of the class barely moved, the twins sensed a wave of revulsion pass through it.

"They get sick."

"How sick?"

Miss Rictus was now staring at the twins, as if these next words were especially for them.

"Their lungs become infected."

"And then?"

"They die, if they do not repent."

"And what happens when they die?"

"They become moonghosts."

There was a collective shudder in the room.

"Yes, Wag, you are right," Miss Rictus said with satisfaction. "And we are all prey to the moonghost, should we ever depart from the Six Precepts. Even I. Even Mr Groak." The latter possibility – though, to Miss Rictus, comically remote – was meant to underline the severity of the threat, but few of the children were taken in by it. "So, I hope our little foreigners are beginning to understand the importance of obedience. Obedience to the Spur."

Numero, son of the Estate of Mathematics, sitting quietly in the front row, suddenly began to cough.

Keiron recognized the racking cough from the previous night. How sickly the boy looked, with his white, waxy face and lanky hair. The class listened in pained silence as Numero tried in vain to quell the convulsions in his chest and the irritation in his throat; it hadn't helped that until then he had used all his willpower to repress the cough while Miss Rictus was speaking.

Cassie knew that she should stay still and silent in her seat, and that if she went to comfort him, Miss Rictus would pounce on her, but she could not help herself. Taking a deep breath, she shot Keiron a glance, then rose and slid quickly up the aisle between the desks to Numero. She slid her arm around his shoulders; but as she began to speak soothingly to him, she felt Miss Rictus's bony hands on her arm.

"Get back to your seat at once," the teacher hissed, her eyes livid. When Cassie hesitated, barely understanding the objection, Miss Rictus wrenched her away and pushed her back towards her desk.

"But he's ill," Cassie protested in amazement. "Can't you see that?"

"There's nothing we can do about that!" Miss Rictus snapped. "Our medicines are no match for it. He is being punished for some transgression which he won't reveal."

"I don't believe it. It's just an illness," Cassie retorted hotly. "I'm sure I can help him."

"*Back to your seat.*" Miss Rictus pointed a long, sharpened nail at the girl, and it was trembling with anger.

Keiron said quietly, "Go back, please, Cassie. You can help him later."

Cassie looked around and saw that all eyes were imploring her to go back to her seat. Those eyes said, "We appreciate your concern, but you don't understand what's going on here, you're only making it worse." Confused, Cassie shrank back to her seat.

Numero's cough subsided and then petered out. He flashed Cassie a grateful glance, then rested his head on the desk, exhausted.

"Do not get up from your desk unless you have permission," Miss Rictus said. Cassie bit back a hostile retort just in time.

"Now, class. We have wasted enough time. This morning, I want you to select one of the *Precepts of Obedience* and construe it."

There was a general opening of desks and shuffling of papers and quills.

"What does construe mean, Miss?" Astar asked, having waited patiently for Miss Rictus to notice that her hand was up. She knew the meaning of the word, of course, but she was asking for the twins' sake.

"I'll construe you, child, every part of your body," Miss Rictus snapped back, not taken in by this ruse. "Until you're laid bare with nothing left to hide in that weed-strewn soul of yours."

They glared at each other until Astar, guessing to the second just how far she could go, lowered her eyes. Being a child of the Estate devoted to the study of Nature in all its forms, animal, vegetable and mineral, the notion of her soul as being *weed-strewn* was hardly the insult it was meant to be, and Astar was, perversely, rather pleased with it; she despised the cultivated.

Keiron found in his desk a dog-eared book entitled *The Six Precepts*. He turned to the chapter on Obedience. There, he found lists setting out long-winded definitions of obedience. He discovered forms of words to use when being obedient in different situations. There was a section entitled, curiously, *Politeness in Body Posture*. The chapter started with a section called *Obedience to Teachers*. Further on, there were more lists: *Obedience to Council Members, Obedience to Citizens*, and so on; each one was accompanied by a list of punishments for transgressions. There was even a mysterious section entitled *Obedience to Oneself*.

Everyone started writing in exercise books. Except the twins. "I suppose I cannot possibly expect our wild and uninitiated incomers to construe anything of this, can I?" Miss Rictus sighed with exaggerated forbearance. She rapped her hand twice on the desk to signal her impatience. "You two," she ordered. "Copy out the first chapter and see that you learn it by heart. You will have to start at the beginning, just as the wretched seven-year-olds have to when they first come here. Well, don't look so stupid, get on with it."

The twins reluctantly settled to the task. They were beginning to feel cowed by Miss Rictus, by the fear that hung invisibly in the air, by the great, gloomy building, its air of being a prison; they scarcely knew how easily they were succumbing to the atmosphere of repression.

I must obey our Headteacher at all times and with the utmost reverence, Keiron wrote, pathetically grateful that his father had insisted on him learning a neat handwriting style.

I must obey my class teacher in every look, word and deed, and be grateful for all that he or she does for me, night and day, Cassie wrote. She paid so much attention to neatness, she scarcely noticed what she was writing, which was perhaps just as well.

Jessie was writing, *One can be obedient to everything outwardly. But this is not enough. If you harbour disobedient thoughts, the fog will attack your lungs. You will get the Cough Terrible and die a slow and horrible death. Then you will become a moonghost, hidden in the fog, looking out for other disobedient ones to fasten on...* At one level, he didn't believe a word of it; but at a deeper level, he was terrified that it might be true. How could one know? So many people died of the Cough. And the mist swirled with creatures that looked like ghosts if you stared hard enough, or if they were caught unawares in a shaft of unexpected moonlight. Yet, on the other hand, he knew there was nothing wicked about Numero; on the contrary, his friend was a gentle boy who cared only about the mystery of numbers. Carefully, Jessie crafted his little essay so that it not only said the right things but made it appear that he believed them too.

A lugubrious old clock on the wall ticked the hours away. The children wrote until their hands ached and their minds were numb with thinking. Miss Rictus knew how to push them to their limits.

"Well," she said at last, breaking the tortured silence. "Let's glance at your feeble efforts, shall we."

She paced slowly up and down the aisle, tapping a long thin ruler in the palm of her hand. Occasionally, the ruler stung an ear in punishment for a spelling mistake, or untidiness, or crossings-out. If a thought was badly expressed or, worse, erroneous, the miscreant had to put out their hand, and down would come the ruler with a sharp slap.

She studied the twins' work with disdain, secretly disappointed that they wrote so fine a hand. "Now learn it," she barked. "You can sit in here on your own this afternoon while the rest of the class are in the workshops. I shall expect you to be able to recite the first chapter word for word by the end of the week."

Everyone was seated at the tables in the dining-room but no one was allowed to eat the watery cheese, dry bread and withered apples that were set before them. All eyes were on the Headmaster, Mr Groak, who had risen in high dudgeon from his place at the top table.

He was a huge, corpulent man. The buttons of his waistcoat strained against the balloon of his belly and his trousers sagged beneath it. The fleshy jowls of his face sprouted billowing tufts of grey hair, and his bald pate gleamed. His eyes were sunk into flesh and seemed to be straining to meet above his ample, pitted, scarlet nose.

"You all know by now that we have strangers in our midst," he said, his voice growling and gravelly. He glared at the twins. "And strangers bring with them the baleful influences of the outside world, like dung on their boots and foul things in their hair."

The twins gasped. Outraged, they rose instinctively, intending to walk out. Never had they been spoken to like this, not even by the arrogant Queen of East Island or even by their great enemy, Prince Badrur.

"Sit down," Mr Groak bellowed, his sideburns trembling.

"Please," whispered Jessie and Astar through unmoving lips.

The twins froze. Their hearts were beating furiously. If only their father could see this; he'd give this Groak a piece of his mind.

"You must sit down," Jessie whispered; and it was more the desperate tone of his voice than anything else which made them think again.

Slowly, they regained their seats.

"As you see, I speak advisedly," Groak continued. He glanced approvingly at Miss Rictus. "For these two are foreigners. They bring with them unruliness and violence. Yes, violence: you are right to look shocked. Last night, Miss Rictus was set upon by this lout..." He pointed an accusing finger at Keiron. "For which, if I had my way, he would be confined to the Dark Room for at least a week."

A few of the less schooled younger children stirred and gasped; one unwisely began to snivel.

"But Miss Rictus has prevailed upon me, in her kindness – a rather misplaced kindness, I think, Miss Rictus, if you don't mind me saying so – to overlook the incident this once. He is a newcomer, scared and ignorant of our civilized ways, she tells me. I'm inclined to think otherwise, but as you all know, Miss Rictus has a soft heart; she has asked me to administer only the mildest of punishments for him."

He pointed accusingly at Cassie, too. "I see sullenness and insolence in that face, too," he shouted, his finger trembling. "You two will leave this room at once. You will not have your meal. You will return to your classroom and learn the *Precepts of Obedience*, for you have dire need of them. Now, go."

The twins rose uncertainly. Cassie began to protest. "But he was only..."

"Don't disgrace us further," Miss Rictus barked. "It is intolerable, after the mercy extended to you, that you should still attempt to question... " Miss Rictus suddenly put her hand to her face in a mock gesture of despair. "Oh, I can hardly bear it, Mr Groak."

"Courage, Miss Rictus. I'm sure you've knocked worse ruffians than these into shape."

He turned to the twins. "Well, what are you waiting for?"

They hurried out, indignant, frightened, outraged that this should be happening to them.

As the tedious and silent hours ticked by in the deserted classroom that afternoon, the twins tried valiantly to learn some of the *Precepts of Obedience*, but the words turned to dust in their mouths.

"If we don't learn them," Cassie sighed with exasperation, "we'll only be punished."

"I'd rather be punished than learn this stuff. It's awful." He fished Will from his pocket, slightly annoyed that the usually so talkative manikin was keeping his head down.

"If it's the sort of thing those poor little seven- and eight-year-olds have drummed into them," said Cassie, casting aside the book, then reluctantly pulling it towards her again, "no wonder they walk around like ghosts. You can see the misery in their faces. It's wicked. I can't think why their parents allow it to happen."

"It's the law. Jessie explained that to me. On this island everyone respects the law and custom and all that. And in his parents' day, there was a head-mistress who was quite kind. Groak's changed every-thing, and because the parents never come here, they don't really know."

"Well, they should listen to their children, and make it their business to know," Cassie declared hotly.

"People keep their heads down here, don't they. No one complains," Keiron sighed. "It's as if the fog has sapped their energies."

The light lessened, and the twins finally gave up on the *Precepts*. It depressed them to think that beyond those deadly lists of obedience stretched further chapters on the five other precepts, no doubt also to be committed to heart.

There was nothing else to do. The door had been locked so they could not explore, and the classroom was devoid of anything remotely interesting. They thought of going through the desks of the other chil-dren, to find out more about them, but that struck them as somehow dishonest. Instead they amused themselves watching Will leap from desk to desk. The space between each desk was for him a chasm, requiring effort and courage; but he eventually made it to Miss Rictus's desk with the biggest jump of all.

He was sitting on a wooden box containing pens and pencils when Miss Rictus herself suddenly appeared. She caught sight of Will before Keiron had time to get to her desk and snatch him up.

"Stay where you are," she ordered Keiron.

In a flash, Will jumped off the box and slithered down the desk leg. He was away, weaving through the desks and out of the door before Miss Rictus could gather her wits and stop him.

"Whatever was that?" she said.

The twins glanced at each other, then looked suitably puzzled. "What was what, Miss Rictus?" Kieron asked innocently.

"Don't play games with me, boy. That – creature."

"We don't know what you mean," said Cassie. "What creature?"

"I know what I saw!" Miss Rictus shouted. She was not used to children thwarting her, let alone playing games with her in so blatant a manner. For a moment she felt she was losing control, and the feeling unnerved her.

"But what did you see?" Keiron asked, throwing out his hands theatrically. "We didn't see anything, did we, Cass?"

Cassie shook her head solemnly.

Miss Rictus glowered at them. "I'll get to the bottom of this," she warned. She had come in to test them on what they had learnt, but she had been thrown by this; at least Will had saved them from that.

They heard her turn the key in the lock.

Will huddled in the shadows at the foot of the stairs to the first floor and watched Miss Rictus sweep past, muttering furiously to herself. He looked up the stairs; perhaps the best thing was to make his way to the dormitory where he would be bound to meet up with

Keiron again that night. It was too risky hanging about outside the classroom, where he might be discovered or trampled on by passing feet. But the flight of wooden stairs looked too steep and exhausting, especially after his gymnastics in the classroom; he thought he'd rest for a while.

He found a hiding place and dozed, waking to the boom of the gong through the building. He heard the sound of approaching regiments of feet: time to run. He fled downwards, jumping from step to step in a panic, and reached the basement. But still the pound of many feet followed him, and he hurried down a long, dark corridor away from the dining-hall. To the left were the kitchens. He veered to the right, ran through winding passageways thick with dust, and found himself tumbling down a narrow little stairway. He thumped against a door at the bottom.

He lay there for a while, winded and dazed.

He became aware of a little hole in the bottom of the door, caused by rot in the damp wood. He wriggled through it. He entered a shadowy room, circular and empty. A large mosaic in the floor described a circle divided into twelve segments, one of which, mysteriously, was obscured with a thick layer of dust. In each segment was a picture and a word. Will puzzled over the meaning of these, until he linked them with the Eleven Estates and their individual themes. There was Jessie's, for instance, showing the storytelling chair with the word "storytelling" written above it. But why twelve segments, he wondered, instead of eleven?

He kicked at the dust in the obscured segment, blew at it, and swished it away with his hands, creating a great cloud of it around him. When it had settled, and he'd brushed it from his eyes and ears, he read what it said in the segment: *Magic*. He scuffed further and uncovered a picture of a beautiful, misty-blue castle full of towers and turrets. He imagined walking through its light-filled rooms and corridors, and heard the swish of wings, the neigh of horses. This is where the Diamond Horse lives, he thought. And this is where the twins should be.

CHAPTER 4

That same night, on the far eastern coast, a ship, battered and broken on heavy seas, was being blown out of control towards rocks just beneath the waves. It had made a long and hair-raising voyage from East Island, lashed by torrential rain, surviving storms and treacherous waves, fighting off attacks by huge sea monsters; but now, having reached its destination, it was a ghost of itself, ready to succumb to the implacable sea.

It had a strange crew: one man, young, fiercely proud and determined, whom not even the seas and the heavens could thwart, and a bedraggled collection of scorpion-men. Half the latter had perished at sea; the rest were panicking.

The ship listed. The scorpion-men clung to the rail, screaming.

A great, cold wave crashed over the deck.

There was a deep cracking sound, as if the backbone of the ship was breaking. The last mast fell, and the ship listed almost ninety degrees. Scorpion-men plunged screaming into the seething waters and were swallowed up in the waves.

The young man clung grimly to the wheel. He waited for the crucial moment, just before the boat began to sink. Then he hurled himself clear and struck out away from the ship with all his remaining strength. He was lucky: a wave picked him up and carried him away.

Looking back, he could just see through the spray the prow of the ship sliding into the sea. The last of the scorpion-men were sucked down with it.

He struck out towards the shore, and the waves carried him forward. They threw him on to a stony beach. He crawled forward out of the reach of their cold, sucking fingers, and collapsed.

When he woke, he was shivering. The fog swirled around him, and the sea thundered close by. He staggered up from the beach and into a forest.

The sound of the sea faded, and the fog cleared among the trees a little. He strode on, shaking off his shivering, feeling invigorated by the walk on firm land. He did not give a second thought to his dead crew or his lost ship. This is where he needed to be. The Golden Spurs were here. And old scores needed to be settled.

Prince Badrur had arrived on West Island. He had come with hatred in his heart for the twins and their father. He had come with a burning desire for the Spurs.

Guided by a wooden signpost, he followed a shingle track that eventually led to the gate in the wall Tancred and the twins had passed through days earlier.

He paused at the steps to the main entrance of the house. He had no idea what reception he would have here. Probably they would be hostile to strangers. On his own for the first time, he felt uncharacteristically defenceless, and he decided to scout around the house first. All the rooms he crept past on the right of the house seemed deserted, although lamps flickered in them. At the back of the house, cooking smells led him to the kitchen, and he suddenly realized how hungry and thirsty he was. Peering in, he was surprised to see that it was empty, too. There was the half-eaten carcass of a roasted bird on the table, some bread and flagons of drink. He seized on these and devoured the food, tearing the meat from the carcass and swigging down great gulps of water.

He expected at any minute to be interrupted and challenged, but no one disturbed him. The silence of the place, the mysterious air of sudden desertion, began to intrigue him. Where was everyone?

He crept like a thief through the house. At the foot of the stairs he could hear a voice droning on, not in conversation, but in one long, monotonous utterance. He crept up the stairs and peered through a window in the door.

A crowd of people were listening to a storyteller. She, more richly dressed than most of the others, held them spellbound with her tale. He studied with interest their elongated ears and their strange wide-looking eyes. They all wore the same simple tunics, except for the storyteller and those sitting either side of her, who wore long green gowns glittering with sequinned patterns.

The woman – Marsia – came to the end of her tale and received prolonged applause. "More. More," the audience demanded.

"You are too kind," Marsia protested, bowing and smiling.

Centuries of fog had thrown the people of the Island together in such a way that storytelling had become their chief delight and pastime. Every towns-person or Estate worker had a repertoire of stories to tell, usually passed down in their families. But the best stories were told on this Estate, as was to be expected, and some of the listeners would be sent to other estates to spread the art. But Badrur was not to know this: all he saw was a gathering of people idling their time away.

"Just one more then," she said. "Has anyone any suggestions?"

"What about the Horse of the Eclipse?" cried one. "They say the eclipse will soon be upon us."

That caused many an anxious murmur.

"Please," another shouted. "Let us hear of the coming of the Dark Rider. We haven't heard that one for a long time." The murmurs increased.

She glanced at Torke. He shrugged, as if to say, "Why not?"

She settled back into her chair and closed her eyes, summoning up the story reluctantly from hidden depths. This was a story that always sent a shiver through her.

"The dark side of the moon was jealous," she began. Her voice was so solemn, her listeners fell silent. "Jealous of the beautiful Diamond Horse that had been made from the light side of the moon. There came the blackest of eclipses here on this island, as if the moon had been reversed. Out of the blackness, an evil hand fashioned a horse, a horse with wings, as black as night. The Horse of the Eclipse."

The audience shifted uncomfortably. Children huddled closer to their parents.

"You all know about the Horse of the Eclipse. Wherever it lands, there death visits. One touch of its black wing and you become a moonghost. Look into its eyes and you lose your soul..."

Badrur's heart quickened. What a creature!

"On its forehead is a drop of the deepest, densest darkness. It may look like nothing more than a drop of jet: don't be fooled by that. Concentrated inside it is all the life-denying essence of the eclipse itself." She swept the audience with a look so grave, people felt a shadow pass over them.

She was silent for a moment.

"If the Horse of the Eclipse finds its Dark Rider," she said, almost in a whisper. "It will be more powerful even than the Diamond Horse..."

She paused for dramatic effect. Torke, unable to restrain himself, interpolated significantly, "For remember, the Diamond Horse still awaits its Rider, and without its Rider it has only half its strength."

Marsia nodded solemnly. "And the Horse of the Eclipse will come among us like a dark plague, robbing the moonhorses of their goodness and leaving us prey to the moonghosts. We shall all die of the Cough Terrible..."

"No!" someone shouted.

"Never!" shouted another.

She held up her hand, and when the audience had grown calm again, she described how the Dark Rider and his horse would lay waste the Eleven Estates. Her husband glanced at her with increasing concern, wondering why she was intent on frightening her audience tonight. She couldn't help herself, she was in the grip of the story, it had to be seen to its end. Such were her powers of description, she worked her audience into a frenzy of protest and fear.

"But there is a worse fate awaiting us," she cried, holding up her hand to be heard, "which is even more bloodcurdling than this. I can barely bring myself to utter it." The audience urged her to the story's climax. "If the Horse of the Eclipse is ridden by the Dark Rider wearing the Golden Spurs. . ." she cried, holding up her arms as if to embrace the night.

But she let the people's fate hang in the air, her words no match for the dark and lurid fantasies of death, disease and destruction, of enslavement and eternal misery, kindled in their minds.

Badrur himself had been caught up in the excitement of the story. He imagined himself as the Dark Rider astride the Horse of the Eclipse, and it filled him with desire and exaltation. He could hold himself back no longer. He threw open the double doors to the hall and strode in. In that heightened atmosphere, his sudden appearance was like an apparition. To the people who turned to stare at him, it was as if he had stepped out of the dark swirlings of their imaginations, an image of the Dark Rider himself. In truth, he was a startling sight. His hair was long, black, straggly, framing a dead white face and brilliant black eyes. His long coat, his once bright tunic and his trousers were torn and streaked with seawater. And his ears and eyes were those of a foreigner's.

He swept around the front to face them, and stood between Jessie's father and mother, who fell back, as afraid as the rest of them.

"Let me tell you who I am," he said, commanding instant attention, "Prince Badrur, son of the Queen of East Island."

At the mention of his name, there was a great stir. Marsia and Torke glanced anxiously at one another. They all remembered what Tancred and the twins had told them about this man.

"I have come here, across the most treacherous seas, to tell you my story. I have come to tell you what happened when I tried to find the Helmet and the Shield of the famed and wondrous Golden Armour."

"We've heard your story already," Torke interrupted a little nervously.

Badrur shot him an impatient and quizzical glance. "How can that be?"

Ah, so I am on their track already, he thought, once he heard the reason. "Well," he said, there's always at least two sides to every story. Let me tell you how it really happened. If you don't mind?"

"This is the Estate of Storytelling," said Torke. "Stories are given many outings here. Go ahead."

Gradually, as he unfolded his version of the hunts for the Helmet and the Shield, casting himself as the hero and giving himself the most irreproachable motives, he erased in the audience's mind the impression they had formed at his entry, that he was somehow in league with the Horse of the Eclipse. He coaxed and charmed them until they were dazzled.

Torke and Marsia, despite his eloquence, were not taken in by him, but they thought it best to offer him a room for the night.

He requested a hookah and a mix of some special ground seeds and herbs which he liked to smoke, and was eventually left alone to stare out of his window where the fog swirled in the darkness, creating fantastic shapes. His hair clean, his beard shaven, new linen against his skin, a green robe to replace his old black one, and the fumes of the herbs in his nostrils: suddenly, despite the fact that he had lost everything with the sinking of his ship, he was happy. Visions of the Horse of the Eclipse emerging out of the moon's darkness and riding like thunder over the land, *with him on its back*, filled his inflamed mind.

He woke to a misty light. As he stood by the window, contemplating what he might do that day, Jessie's moonhorse wandered in and out of the fog in the garden below him, pausing to nibble the grass. Her wings were folded, and for a few minutes Badrur could not make out what they were – not until, in fact, the moonhorse flapped them to shake off the damp. A flying horse!

He ran down the stairs and out into the fog.

The moonhorse flapped her wings to clear the fog around her. Badrur approached her carefully. She watched him apprehensively, then began to back away. But she made the mistake of looking into his eyes.

Badrur had been born with the gift of hypnotism. He could switch on a beam of light in his eyes which put the creatures of the animal kingdom in his power. As a boy he had made the animals and birds of the forest dance and fight for his amusement. As a man, he had commanded a legion of monsters on North Island. A flying horse was no match for him.

The moonhorse felt her resistance melt away. She lowered her head and stepped towards him. Badrur stroked her and murmured soothing things to her. To the uninitiated, it looked like a man merely patting a horse. But to the moonhorse, his touch was a great degradation.

With a powerful leap, Badrur jumped on to her back.

At the same moment, several people from the house appeared out of the fog and surrounded him. When they saw him on the moonhorse's back, they could scarcely believe their eyes.

"Stop, stop this at once," Marsia cried in acute distress. "No one is allowed to ride the moonhorse except our son. It is sacrilegious. Please get down at once."

Badrur shook his head good-humouredly.

"You must!" Torke demanded furiously, advancing on the prince. "The moonhorse is sacred. Only the Children of the Estates can ride them. All else pollute them. Get down at once."

But it was clear Badrur had no intention of doing so.

Suddenly, at a signal from Marsia, the crowd swarmed around the horse and pulled Badrur from her back. He kicked out, cursing, and fought wildly against this indignity, but the crowd subdued him.

The moonhorse neighed, and galloped off into the fog, fear flaming in her mind. It would be many days before the power of Badrur's hypnotic eyes wore off, and until then she hid in the undergrowth like a wounded animal.

"You have profaned a moonhorse," Torke pronounced, a look of such severity on his face, all fell silent. He held up a hand to forestall Badrur's protest. "Ignorance is no defence. You will be taken before the Council, there to answer for your misdeed."

Two guards seized him.

"Take him to the city at once," Torke commanded.

The two guards were hardly sufficient to hold Badrur for long. When night fell and his hands were untied so that he could feed himself, he slipped a slender knife from inside his boot and with one swift movement, he slit the throat of the nearest guard. The other tried to flee, but Badrur hurled the knife at him: it sank between his shoulder blades.

Badrur trod purposefully down the shingle road that cut through the forest towards the city. Satisfaction at disposing of the guards lessened his anger at being ejected from the estate. If he could only get his hands on another moonhorse, he thought, he could travel the island at will.

He heard a crashing through the undergrowth, and guessing it was a large animal, he shinned up a tree and waited. A powerful deer-like creature emerged from the trees and trotted down the road. Just before it passed below him, he jumped down into its path. It reared and bellowed in fright, but his hypnotic gaze had locked on to it before it could tear itself away.

Now he had a mount, alas not one with wings, but it would do.

He reached the city about noon on the following day.

Leaving his mount at the edge of the forest, he slipped unseen into the shrouded city. The roofs of the tall grey buildings were lost in the fog, and the narrow cobbled streets dissolved into walls of shifting grey. Townspeople hurried past like phantoms.

Badrur peered through lighted windows to get a sense of how the people lived. In some rooms, they sat silent, daydreaming; or else they gathered in knots to exchange stories. Some people strummed zither-like instruments and sang songs so mournful it made him want to grind his teeth. A few rooms showed small children gathered around tables, reading or writing, as if at a private school; and there were workshops in which adults toiled. From time to time, he saw spurs hanging from walls and beams, and these intrigued him.

He guessed there was some centre of power here – there always was where people were gathered; but how to find it? He asked a few times, but the people he stopped looked startled or wary and slid away into the fog without answering him. He cursed them loudly and walked on.

An old woman emerged from a tall, narrow terraced house as he passed, and he asked her too.

"I am going there myself," she muttered reluctantly. "It is the day when they open the Sanctuary to this sector of the city. You may accompany me, if you like."

"The Sanctuary? What is that?"

She paused and looked at him slyly. "Another stranger?"

"Yes, I come from East Island. Have there been others, then?"

She shuffled on, not answering. He jumped in front of her and opened his arms to stop her. "Well?"

"Out of my way," she grumbled, waving her hand about in agitation. Then she stopped and burst into a racking cough which shook her frail body and doubled her up with pain.

He followed her through the fogbound streets until they came to the Square. He paused to admire one of the statues of the moonhorses, and in doing so, he lost her in the fog. Crossing the Square, he came across the mosaic of the Spurs, and his heart quickened. He was reminded of a game he used to play with Angharer, his aunt who had brought him up as a child: she would hide an object and he had to look for it; the nearer he got to it, the "hotter" he was; the further away, the "colder" he was. Well, staring down at this mosaic he felt "warm", if not "hot", and the childish thought made him chuckle.

He found a queue of people shuffling into a side entrance to the great building on one side of the Square, and he joined it. Just ahead of him was the old woman who had led him there. She was talking in low tones to an acquaintance. He picked up a few of her words, and was soon listening with rapt attention.

"The Councillor would not tell me who they were," she was saying. "Foreigners, of course; they have such funny ears and small eyes. Have you ever seen any foreigners?" Her friend shook her head. "The children were like two versions of the same face. Have you ever seen a boy and girl that looked the spitting image of each other?" Her friend shook her head again. "Nor me. Perhaps it's more common on the other islands. Anyway, when I told them about the school, you should have seen their faces! They've never been to a school, you see. They thought, being foreigners, they'd be able to escape it! Huh, I said, that's one thing you'll never get out of on this island. It's almost as sacred as the Spur."

"I quite enjoyed school," said her friend. "Once I'd learnt all the Precepts. I was never very good at remembering things." Her face took on a reflective look.

"I hear tell that Mr Groak is strict," said the old woman. "And that Miss Rictus. Some parents don't like it, but what can they do? The school's always been a law unto itself."

"Children getting too soft, more like," said her friend, echoing a common misconception.

They were moving at a snail's pace down a long tunnel. Several people were coughing, some doubled up with the effort of it, but no one seemed to take note of it except Badrur, who found it puzzling. The tunnel led into a furnished chamber and up a wide flight of carpeted stairs. At the top were huge open double doors. Guards flanked the stairs and filtered the people into the Sanctuary.

He put up the hood on his robe to hide his ears, and he kept his head bent as he climbed the stairs. He received some curious glances, but he was still wearing the robe he was given on the estate, and the guards recognized its distinctive colour and design and didn't challenge him.

The file of people moved slowly around a cordoned-off area in the centre of a vast room. On an elaborate plinth, covered with a highly embroidered cloth, was a large glass pendant suspended from a stand made of what looked like moonstone or mother of pearl. Badrur was within a few feet of it before he realized what was encased inside the glass pendant; the knowledge shot through him like a bolt of lightning. He stumbled and gasped. A guard standing nearby moved to help him but he waved him away.

In the glass pendant was the left Golden Spur. It radiated its own soft, golden light, like a muted candle. It was no bigger than a child's hand. Badrur could see an intricate design etched in the gold. There were six spokes to the spur wheel, and precious stones clustered in the wheel's hub. It was more like a magnificent piece of jewellery than an object of war; but he was oblivious to its beauty: to him it represented a power and a magic which he would give everything to possess, to bend to his own ambitions. His desire for that Spur was so great, he trembled at the effort it took to stop himself lunging forward to snatch it.

As soon as they were outside, he grabbed hold of the old woman. "Where is the other Spur?" he demanded, his eyes fierce with avarice. The old woman complained loudly and tried to shake him off; she attracted a little crowd. "Where is the other Spur?" he shouted. His hood had fallen and they could see he was a foreigner.

A burly man stepped forward and made him release the old woman. "She doesn't know. None of us do. If we did, don't you think it would be in the Sanctuary too?"

Controlling his impatience, Badrur said, "But you must have some idea. There must be stories about it."

"There are always stories here," said the burly man.

"Tell me," he pleaded.

But they were on their guard.

"We don't know where it is," the burly man said with finality. "And you shouldn't ask."

"Why not?"

"It's not for us to know."

The little crowd melted away into the fog.

He cursed them under his breath. Nothing enraged Badrur more than to be frustrated in his purpose. Behind him was one of the Spurs, so heavily guarded it would take an earthquake or a miracle to steal it. And without the other Spur, it might not be of much use anyway. How bitter-sweet!

He debated what to do next.

Go to the school? That's where those meddlesome twins were, if he understood the old woman's gossip correctly. If anyone had a clue to the whereabouts of the other Spur, it would be them. He would have to find them and squeeze it out of them, or at least shadow them: that surely was his best move.

Across the Square, he passed one of the statues of the moonhorses. Its profile rose proudly in the shifting of fog. He had the urge to mount it, but as its flank was taller than he was, it would take a giant leap to do it.

He became aware of two small children sitting underneath the horse, leaning against its hind legs. They were watching him with wide, wary eyes.

"Tell me," he said. "Have you ever ridden a moon-horse?"

They shook their heads, aghast at the suggestion.

"But you will do one day, won't you?"

They shook their heads again, and backed away, frightened at what he was saying. From the earliest age, they knew the moonhorses were sacred.

"Why not?"

"We're not Children of the Estates," said one.

"We're not twelve," said the other.

Badrur took note of both answers.

"Soon," he said, "you'll be going to the school, won't you?"

They nodded. He noticed them stiffening at the thought.

"Where is the school?"

"Across the lake," said one.

"And where's the lake?"

"Over there," said the other, pointing vaguely.

And then, as if their courage in talking to this stranger had reached its limits, they glanced swiftly at each other and fled.

Badrur finally reached the shores of the lake the following evening. A wind had blown up and was shifting the fog that hung about the lake and the school. He caught glimpses of the sprawling dark building on the island through long coiling strands of fog. He was lucky to find a tethered boat, and he rowed it across the choppy water. Inside that building were the twins. It gave him pleasure to think of them incarcerated in such a forbidding place, separated, as he guessed, from their father. Somehow or other, given how the goddess Citatha had helped them find the Helmet and the Shield, they would in time lead him to the missing Golden Spur.

CHAPTER 5

Mr Groak had been Headmaster of the school for only the last few years. In that time, he had slowly tightened his grip on the discipline of the place, getting rid of teachers he thought too kind, too understanding, and replacing them with others more akin to his own strict view of life. He regarded Miss Rictus as a model member of staff, if a little fawning. His method was to make changes in small degrees, by stealth, so that hardly anyone but the children would notice, at least not so much as to complain. It had worked beautifully. After all, children always complained about school: who would seriously listen to them?

Arrogance ran in his veins, his grey eyes glinted severity, and his pudgy hands twisted incessantly with impatience.

Yet here he was, sitting opposite this tall, pale, dark haired young man with fierce eyes and coils of black hair down to his shoulders, feeling as if some ancient carpet, which he had trodden for half a century, had suddenly been wrenched from his feet, revealing a gaping hole in the floor before him. He trembled inwardly; but what scared him most was that he did not know why he trembled. Why should this young man, with his mocking lips and insinuating voice, cause such terror in his heart? He wiped his mouth and tried to keep his gaze steadily fixed on Badrur's face.

Badrur was well aware of the effect he had on the headmaster; as soon as he had been shown to Groak's study and had seized the old man's hand to shake, he was aware of a cowardly and corrupt soul, and he knew he had found a useful, if despicable, ally. Of course, Groak had tried to disapprove of his coming, saying it was strictly against the rules, but Badrur had fixed him with those powerful eyes of his and silently swept the objection aside.

"I will get straight to the point, Mr Groak," he said, powerfully squeezing the man's damp hand. "I have come to this island – indeed, I have been *sent* here by forces I do not wish to specify, if you understand me..." Groak nodded, pretending he did, "...to find the missing Golden Spur. And I believe you can help me."

Groak, startled, detached his hand. "But that's impossible!" he protested. He poured himself a drink to steady himself. "Why me? Why here?"

"Why you?" Badrur echoed, as if to say, Who else should I come to for such a dark and dangerous quest? He meant to use flattery, and he could see that it was already beginning to work. He threw out dark hints about destiny, and eclipses, and historic forces, and the chosen few, until Groak's head was spinning. It wasn't long before Badrur had him eating out of his hand. They settled down to plot like two old cronies, nursing their drinks and speaking in whispers.

"There is also the matter of the brats," Badrur explained. "Children of Lord Tancred from North Island. You have them here, I believe?"

Groak scowled. "We have them here all right. Nothing but a damn nuisance. They stir up discontent in their class, which is difficult enough to control at the best of times. But it won't be long before we break their spirits."

"I have no love for them, either," Badrur said bitterly. "But I would ask you not to send them mad with your little tortures. I may have need of them."

"You?"

Badrur leaned forward to emphasize his point. "Those two have an uncanny knack of being where the missing pieces of Armour are. They led me to the Helmet. They found the Shield."

Groak's eyes widened. "Really? I thought that was all just fanciful stories. They look very ordinary to me."

Badrur shook his head. "Believe me, they're not!" He said significantly, "My guess is, they are the ones who will lead me to the missing Spur."

They were interrupted by a knock on the door, and Miss Rictus entered. She hesitated on the threshold.

"Come in, Mildred, come in," Groak gestured impatiently. "We have with us a most distinguished visitor. Let me introduce you to Prince Badrur, son to the Queen of East Island."

Royalty! Miss Rictus looked into Badrur's eyes and was instantly awed, not to say quelled. She stammered, put out her hand, then withdrew it in confusion. Badrur sized her up in one glance – her mean little eyes, her bullying heart, her sycophancy – and saw in her another potential ally. He flattered her with little gestures, showing her to a seat, fetching her a drink, making absurd compliments, until her grey eyelashes began to flutter nervously. A little later, she had calmed sufficiently to be able to answer his questions about the twins. Had they said anything about the Golden Spur? Or their purpose in coming here? She shook her head: she had no idea how important they were, otherwise she would have arranged a permanent watch on them.

"Then you must do it, Miss Rictus," he demanded. "They may let slip something vital."

"It is not easy," she muttered. "The brats in that class stick together. Usually you'll find one or two who are only too glad to act the spy for a little extra ration, or for a hint of kindness, but not this group. They're different. But I'll try." She flashed the prince an ingratiating look.

"Why are they different?" Badrur asked, quick to pick up on the essential point.

She scowled. "They stick together. They watch out for each other."

Groak unfolded a map of the island.

"Ah!" Badrur exclaimed, pointing to a spot on the north-eastern coast, "I have heard about this tower. *The Tower of the Eclipse*. Tell me what you think will happen there when the eclipse happens."

Groak and Miss Rictus glanced at one another and shuddered.

"I hear the eclipse will come soon," he added.

"And out of the sky will come the Horse of the Eclipse," Miss Rictus murmured. "He comes looking for his Dark Rider." She paused; her mouth fell open. No, it couldn't be...

"And who do you think this Dark Rider is?" he smiled, his eyes flaring with arrogance.

Was he serious? They couldn't tell. But the look in his eyes made them tremble.

Badrur rose and said, "I shall set out for the Tower tomorrow. But before I go, I will take a look at these twins. Just to make sure."

Miss Rictus led him along the corridors and up the stairs, nervously carrying her lamp.

He peered at Keiron's sleeping face and sneered. How he had grown to hate it!

When Miss Rictus opened the door of the girls' dormitory, Cassie, barely asleep, stirred and opened her eyes. She screamed.

Had she seen him there, or had she dreamt it? The uncertainty kept her awake all night.

As Badrur had been rowing over the lake to the school, Lord Tancred had set out with a posse of guards and servants, to the Estate of Nature, the first of the Estates to the east of the city, where he was to start his enforced storytelling tour. He felt angry and despondent and his temper with his hosts was prickly. He missed his children, and his heart ached at the thought of what they might be going through at the hands of people who undoubtedly did not know or value them. He knew that, despite what he had said to them, his first duty was to try and release them from the place. He had pleaded much, and made promises, he had cajoled and threatened the members of the Council, but they had merely shrugged their shoulders in sympathy: the rule of custom and law here was not to be trifled with, however pressing the personal claim. Besides, they argued, a spell at school would hardly do his children any harm.

The party toiled up a hill and paused to rest their horses on the brow. The fog swirled around them, caught in strong winds that were sweeping in from the sea and over the treetops. Occasionally, the wind succeeded in breaking the veil of fog, to reveal a glimpse of the city behind them and the vast stretches of the forest in front of them. To their left was the lake and the school. When it appeared briefly in a break in the fog, Tancred felt a stab of such anguish, he nearly cried out. He thought he saw someone rowing alone across the lake to the school. *That could be me!* he thought; and he vowed that before the day was out, it would be him.

They descended once more into the fogbound trees. Imperceptibly, Tancred edged himself to the front of the posse. As soon as the fog came between him and the next rider, he gave them the slip, turning left into the trees and hiding there until they had passed.

The journey to the lake was difficult. Trees hindered him at every step, branches pulled at him, thorns scratched; and he often felt hopelessly lost. It was nightfall before he heard the water at the lake's edge splashing against the bank. He urged his horse through the tall grass along the bank, looking for a boat that might take him across to the school, but there were none except those that looked as if they had been abandoned and would surely sink into the inky waters.

He tethered his horse and sat on the bank. Far from home, without his children, a virtual prisoner, on a seemingly hopeless quest: he chuckled grimly to himself as he assessed his position.

He must have fallen asleep, for he woke with a start to the sound of oars splashing rhythmically in the waters. The fog shifted and swirled, assuming fantastic and ghostly shapes, as if teasing him; only his ears told him of the progress of the boat, and he stumbled along the bank to keep it in earshot. Then a break in the fog revealed a figure rowing vigorously towards the bank. All he could see was a silhouette, but he knew instantly who it was.

The last time he had seen Prince Badrur, his great enemy, was on East Island, being carried up and away half-conscious by flying scorpion-guards. He had hardly given him a thought since, except as the villain in the stories he had told. It was a shock to see him in the flesh again, so near; and why was he here, rowing away from the school, except to prey on the twins?

Sickened, and in a rage, Tancred blundered along the bank, thinking to challenge Badrur when he landed. But instead he ran straight into the guards who were scouting nearby in search of him. Politely they insisted that he resume his journey.

"But all I want is to see my children!" he protested.

"No parent can see their children except on Fogless Day. You know that. Why should you be different?"

Badrur heard the voices, but not knowing who was there, he slid across the water and banked further along the shore.

* * *

Unaware of all these comings and goings, Keiron lay in his bed listening to Numero coughing. The others, he supposed, were used to it and could sleep through it, but Keiron was so attuned to the racking sound, he could almost feel it in his own chest. He felt acutely sorry for the boy.

After a particularly painful bout of coughing, Keiron thought he heard Numero sob, just once, then stifle it. It was too much for him. He got up and crept over to Numero's bed.

"It's me, Keiron," he whispered.

"Hello," Numero whispered back, gratefully. "I'm sorry if I'm keeping you awake."

"Haven't they given you anything for that cough?"

"Yes, Herbie gives me medicine. He's from the Estate of Medicine. But nothing that does any real good."

"Don't they know what causes it?"

"Oh, the fog. Everyone knows that. It gets to some people. And it's got nothing to do with what you're like as a person. That stuff that Rictus comes out with, it's all rubbish."

"Of course it is."

Numero coughed again. It sounded so raw.

"I'm going to get my sister," Keiron said. "She'll help you."

Keiron slipped out and softly knocked on the girls' dormitory door. Cassie heard it at once, slipped out of bed and opened it a crack.

"You've got to come, Cassie," he whispered urgently. "Numero is coughing his heart up. If something isn't done soon..."

Some of the other girls heard him and sat up.

Cassie followed her brother into the boys' dormitory and crouched at Numero's bedside. The boy was silent now, lying on his back. Someone had lit a lamp, and the light caught the sweat on his face.

"Numero, listen to me," Cassie said softly. "I am a healer. I can mend broken bones and heal wounds. I've never tried to fight a disease before, but I want to try. Will you let me?"

Numero stared into her strangely glittering eyes and nodded wonderingly.

Everyone was watching now: the boys stood around the bed, the girls were peering over their shoulders.

Cassie sat beside Numero and laid her hands on his chest. He shivered, for her hands were cold on his feverish skin. She felt the familiar gathering of energy inside her, felt it flow rapidly down into her hands and through her fingers. His body arched slightly as the energy made contact, then it relaxed.

A minute ticked by. Everyone remained still, concentrating on Cassie's hands or Numero's face.

The boy smiled. "It's happening," he whispered. "The pain is going. It feels like it's draining away. Incredible." He closed his eyes. "Oh, I can't believe it."

A whisper of excitement passed through the watching children.

"It's happening!"

But Cassie was less satisfied. She could see, in her mind's eye, the energy flowing like liquid over the dark patches on his lungs and dissolving them, but the usual clarity that she expected to follow it was not there. Instead, there were coils of fog shifting and tangling, forming and fading, inside him. She watched them in dread. One particular coil appeared to form two hollow eyes. Like a ghost. A moonghost.

She pulled her hands away abruptly and shuddered. The moonghost had stared right into her, had made her feel desolate. She shuddered. Perhaps she had imagined it.

No one but Keiron noticed the abruptness of her withdrawal. Their eyes were upon Numero. He was sitting up, grinning, his eyes alight.

"It's gone!" he shouted. "It really has! I don't feel anything there, now. That terrible itch in my chest... I can't believe it." He flung his arms around Cassie and hugged her tightly. "Thank you, thank you," he gasped in relief.

When he let go, Cassie looked into his eyes and said, "I've got rid of the symptoms, Numero. But I'm not sure that the disease has gone yet."

"Of course it has," Numero protested, doubt flickering across his joyful face. "Hasn't it?"

Cassie glanced at Keiron and saw him shake his head ever so slightly.

"Well, perhaps it it has," she smiled. "But take care, Numero, won't you, in case it gets a hold again."

"I shan't need to worry if you're here," he smiled, and he hugged her impulsively again.

Later, as Cassie lay in the dark, she could not get out of her mind that vision of the moonghost inside the boy. It was as if it had fastened itself on him and was slowly sapping the life from him. She had heard from the girls that the Cough Terrible, as they called it, was rife in the city, that people died young of it, and that there was no cure. Moonghosts sucked out the life of wicked people, they had been told time and again by the school, and they were terrified at any sign in their own bodies of coughs, of breathlessness, of pains in the chest. Some of them already suspected that a moonghost was hovering around them, waiting for the first chance to infiltrate, and they stifled each cough with horror.

They saw in Cassie a saviour. They had all insisted in hugging her, touching her, lauding her, after Numero's miraculous cure. But now, as she lay doubting in her bed, she could only sigh. She felt instinctively that she wasn't up against a simple disease here. Something else was at work, too. Something evil. Perhaps the school spoke the truth. Perhaps moonghosts really did exist.

Astar slipped over to her bed in the night and lit a candle. She leaned over Cassie and said, "You're still worried, aren't you? About Numero?"

Cassie nodded.

"There *are* moonghosts, you know," Astar whispered. "I've seen them in the fog. Most of the others try to think of them as stories, told to frighten them. Not that I blame them." She paused. "You saw one, didn't you? In Numero?"

Cassie nodded.

"But it doesn't mean he's bad."

"Of course it doesn't," said Cassie.

"We mustn't tell him. Let him think he's cured."

"So you don't think he is?"

Astar shook her head.

"Then is everyone at the mercy of these moonghosts?"

"We all are. Even you."

"That's terrible."

Astar put her face very close to Cassie's and whispered, "But don't worry. You proved yourself tonight. We all saw that. We are sure now that you are one half of the missing Ancient Rider."

"Half of what?"

"I won't tell you now. I can't, not until..."

She rose to go, as if regretting that she had already said too much.

"Until what?" Cassie demanded, clasping her arm.

"Until Keiron has proved that he is the other half. Now, I have said too much. Keep it to yourself. Sleep well, Cassie."

But Cassie didn't sleep well. How could she?

Later, she connected it with what Will had said, about the mysterious segmented circle in the floor. They had thought he was being typically fanciful and teasing when he told them about it; but now, she thought, was there a link between what Astar had said and the circle in the basement room?

The twins swallowed their impatience and disdain, and learnt the *Precepts of Obedience*. Miss Rictus tested them one afternoon alone in the classroom, her ruler ready to rap across knuckles the minute either of them slipped up. But the twins were determined not to give her that satisfaction and they had schooled themselves well. They trotted out the Precepts parrot-fashion. Finding no fault with that, though annoyed with the deliberate monotony of their tone, Miss Rictus tried to trip them up with random questions about the Precepts, but their recall was adequate for that too.

At the end, she nodded sourly, tapped her ruler in her hand, and said, "Well, this is certainly an improvement on your first days here. I am glad to see the school is having a beneficial effect on you both. Of course, I'm only too aware that you have trotted out the Precepts as if they were no more than nursery rhymes to you. I shall be more impressed when I see you *abide* by them, see your conduct being *ruled* by them. There is still too much insolence in your eyes."

She glared at them, as if goading them to prove her point with some protest or gesture, but they were wise to her now and kept straight, impassive faces. They sensed, too, that she was keeping her natural bullying bridled, though they did not know why; since her meeting with Badrur, she had approached them with a kind of grudging respect and wariness.

"Miss Rictus, may I ask you something?" Keiron asked politely.

"If you must."

"We've heard so much about the workshops. Can we not see them now?"

Miss Rictus returned to her desk and put her ruler away. "You may visit them, I suppose," she said, reluctant to make any concessions, "but you're not yet ready to work in any of the main workshops. You will start by learning to make spurs. That's where the seven-year-olds start, learning to make spurs from metal. It is the most basic skill of all."

She took them up to the floor where the workshops were. There were eleven of them (and one other so long disused it had been all but forgotten); set off on either side of a corridor so long it stretched away into darkness. The doors to each workshop were closed, but the sounds of talk, instruction and activity that filled the corridor told the twins they were in full use. They noticed that each workshop had been given a name which was painted above the door. The nearest doors to them said *Medicine* and *Philosophy*.

"The spurs first," she said, opening a door to a large, low-ceilinged room.

Seven- and eight-year-olds, in dirty smocks, with faces smeared with ash and dust, were clustered around benches or braziers, watching teachers demonstrate some intricate work with hot metal, or banging at and bending bits of metal. The room was hot and airless, acrid with the smell of smoke and charcoal, noisy and oppressive. At their entrance, many of the children stopped work and watched them.

"Get back to your work," one of the teachers bellowed, and a boy's ear was clipped for not instantly obeying.

"These two are ready," Miss Rictus announced to the teacher in charge, a burly man with frowning brows and grimy hands. "See that they behave. Any insolence, report to me." She swept out without a further look at them.

The teacher flung filthy aprons at them. They stared in dismay as he laid out before them all the parts of the spur which had to be made and assembled.

"All the parts are made in moulds," he said. He took from a brazier a little copper pot with a long handle and poured molten orange metal from it into a tiny star-shaped tray. This he plunged into cold water with a sharp hiss of steam, and then turned it out when it was cool. "But that's the easy bit," he said. "Now it has to be filed and polished and balanced, and then you will learn to engrave on it the Six Precepts."

They filed and polished scraps of metal all afternoon. It left them feeling hot, dirty, sore and bored. The prospect of doing this each afternoon filled them with dismay.

What a waste of time, Keiron said to Will as he tried to wash the grime from his body. *Where were you this afternoon, by the way? You're keeping quiet.*

I was afraid of those braziers. And this whole place, the fog, no light, no proper trees. . . I'm depressed!

That made Keiron chuckle. *It's so much easier to carve wood.*

Why do they bother?

Bother about what?

Making these metal spurs. They're useless.

Of course they are. It's all superstition.

They're no protection against the moonghosts. Not really.

Oh, you believe in the moonghosts, do you? Like Cassie.

I do! They're everywhere. But keep that golden spur around your neck, Keiron. That's quite different from what they're doing here. It's special. I have a feeling they don't like it.

"So what's in all the other workshops?" Keiron asked Jessie that night. They were sitting on his bed, huddled in a blanket trying to keep warm.

"Well, apart from Storytelling, there's Medicine. It's where we learn about herbs, and how to make potions, and there's... But I could show you!"

"What do you mean?"

"The workshops! No one goes in them at night. At least, I don't think so. Want me to show you around?"

"Is it allowed?"

"Of course not! That's why I want to do it. Shall we?"

"As long as you don't get yourself into trouble."

"Well, you could send Will on ahead to see if all's clear, couldn't you?"

At the top of the stairs Keiron put Will on the floor and the little manikin ran forward and listened at the first two doors. *No one's there.*

The Medicine workshop was full of plants, bottles, pestles and mortars, bowls containing mixtures, liquids and powders. There were anatomy charts and pickled remains and bits of bone strewn about. Recipe books were stacked high, containing recipes for every potion known to the island.

"This is where Herbie spends most of his time. He comes from the Estate of Medicine, and will be its Councillor one day, so he has to be an expert on medicine. He hopes to find a cure for the Cough Terrible."

The Philosophy workshop consisted of nothing but books and a horseshoe arrangement of old desks with a podium and a blackboard at the front. There was a large china head divided up into areas of thought sitting on the desk, staring from sight-less eyes.

"They call it philosophy," Jessie sneered, "but all we learn here are the *Principles*, as they call them, for the thoughts we should have. Every thought that might be our own is taken to pieces here and shown to be false. I hate this workshop."

"Who comes from the Estate of Philosophy?"

"Idé. She's very quiet. You may hardly have noticed her. She keeps her thoughts to herself. She's very clever, though."

They progressed slowly from workshop to workshop – Art, Food, Technology, Music, Law and Order, Reading and Writing, Number and Nature.

The latter was Astar's domain. It was full of wild plants, stuffed animals, beetles in amber, great tomes full of detailed paintings, rocks and shells.

"It's as wild as Astar's hair!" Keiron laughed. "I think I'd like this workshop."

"Yes, but the teachers make even this place dull and pedantic. You wouldn't believe it."

Across the corridor was another door marked *Story-telling*. "This is my workshop," Jessie said, a note of pride in his voice. It was full of books and pictures, models of people and animals, puppets and masks. There was a big chair on a dais at the front. "Here I learn to tell all the stories which the school allows. It's the one place in the school I love. Even the teachers here are quite decent."

But what about this workshop? came Will's voice from afar. He was leaning against the door at the very end of the corridor which Keiron had failed to see in the shadows. *This is where you belong, Keiron. You and Cassie.*

Keiron held the lamp high. There was dust everywhere, and the name above the door was so obscured by cobwebs, he couldn't read it.

"No one uses it," Jessie said. He tried the door, but it was firmly locked. "It's been shut up for as long as anyone can remember. But now that you're here. . ." He looked strangely at Keiron, as if he knew more than he was saying.

"What is this workshop?"

"Send Will up to clean the sign. Then you'll know."

Will leapt from the top of Keiron's head to the architrave and was soon tangled in skeins of dusty cobwebs. After valiant struggles, which made the two boys laugh, he managed to clear away enough of the webs for the name to be read. It said: *Magic*.

"Magic?" Keiron said. "It doesn't mean – you know, conjuring tricks, does it?"

The look of scorn on Jessie's face scotched that idea.

"Then what?"

"Real magic. Like Cassie's healing. Do you have a gift like that?"

Jessie's eyes narrowed slightly, and Keiron had the impression that much hung on his answer. He nodded. "I do," he said. "Ever since I can remember, I can talk, in my head, to the things around me, things that don't have a voice. Like this door, or this threadbare carpet. They all have a story to tell."

Jessie smiled. "That's great! That means this workshop must be yours."

Keiron looked at the door wonderingly. "But don't we have to be Children of the Estates to have a workshop of our own?"

Jessie shook his head mysteriously. "No. You have to be. . . " Whatever he was going to say was on the tip of his tongue, but some last doubt held him back.

"Be what?" Keiron asked exasperated.

"I'm not sure whether to tell you, yet. Not without proof. I will ask the others." He held up his hand to silence Keiron's protest.

They walked slowly back down the corridor, Keiron disturbed at the unexpected lack of trust he sensed in that moment, Jessie almost bursting with what he wanted to reveal.

"It's my birthday in three days' time, remember," Herbie reminded the boys in the dormitory a few nights later. He'd been giving the others the countdown to his birthday for several days now, and each time he said it, instead of causing comic groans and teasing, there was a pause among the others, charged with anticipation. Keiron saw secret smiles and glances. Was there something special about birthdays here?

"Why does he keep reminding us?" he asked Jessie. "Is he afraid we might forget to get him a present?"

Jessie laughed at that suggestion. "There's only one present he's looking forward to."

"What's that?"

Several of the other boys looked at Jessie, wondering if he was going to give it away. He saw Herbie give a slight shake of his head. "We're keeping it as a surprise."

"Oh," Keiron whispered, "you mean. . .?" and he inclined his head meaningfully in Herbie's direction.

Jessie nodded, grinning; but that only made Keiron

feel that he was still missing something. What were they all up to?

Herbie came and sat beside him, his eyes glowing eagerly. "I'm the last of us to be twelve," he said.

"Oh, I see," said Keiron, wondering if he did. He lowered his voice. "Have you guessed what you're going to get?"

Herbie giggled. "I *know* what I'm going to get. And it's the finest present anyone could wish for in the whole world. You'll see."

When his birthday finally arrived, Herbie was given various little homemade presents from his classmates, and some of the girls had been bold enough to persuade a member of the kitchen staff to make a birthday cake. Before Mr Groak had taken over the school, a great fuss had always been made of birthday children. Now, even cakes were banned. But Herbie did not mind. As the day passed, Keiron and Cassie noticed that he was getting more and more excited, talking too much, sighing, laughing at even the most unfunny comments, falling into silences, looking hot and bothered.

Night came at last.

"Don't change," said Jessie to Keiron. "We're going out again at midnight."

"Midnight? What for?"

"So that Herbie can receive his present."

"Really? Whatever is it?"

"Haven't you guessed yet?" Jessie teased.

"No. Cassie says she has, and Will, but neither will tell me. I'm beginning to think I'm the only one who doesn't know."

"You are! I'll give you a clue. It's coming from his Estate."

Ah, thought Keiron, it's a present from his parents.

For all of them, the minutes ticked by slowly, and for Herbie the slowest of all. But when the great clock in the dining-hall began to boom the midnight chimes throughout the slumberous building, the thirteen children stole silently from their dormitory and up the stairs to the roof. There the fog folded around them, cold and clammy on their faces, glistening in tiny drops on their clothes and hair. They formed a horseshoe shape on an expanse of flat roof, with Herbie set apart inside it, and they joined hands. No one spoke. Everyone looked up into the fog and listened.

"I think I know what it's going to be," Keiron whispered to his sister, his heart suddenly beating faster. Why ever hadn't he guessed before?

It could only be one thing at his age, said Will, scornfully.

They heard a faint swishing sound, and the fog began to thin in the air above them. Then came a pool of faint, bluish light, like a large pale moon.

"She's coming," Herbie shouted, all his suppressed excitement bubbling up. He jumped up and down.

A large patch of fog cleared, and out of the dark sky came a moonhorse. Her moonstone beamed light before her, on to their heads and in a pool around her body. She hovered overhead, so that the wind from her great white wings ruffled their hair; then she lowered herself gracefully before them, landing so skilfully her horseshoes barely seemed to touch the roof.

Only the eager-eyed Will noticed anything slightly awkward about that landing; the others simply delighted in her beauty and felt invigorated by her light.

The moonhorse folded her wings and looked straight at Herbie.

He was trembling. His excitement drained away; all he felt was awe. This magnificent and magical beast, that had been in his family for generations, that had been ridden by his father since he was twelve, was to be his? To ride on Fogclear Night through the heavens to the Mooncastle? He could scarcely grasp it. No more being left alone in the dormitory while the others flew off on their moonhorses. No more feeling the odd one out, the one who was too young to be trusted. He was at last to take his rightful place as one of the Ancient Riders.

Astar, seeing that awe had immobilized him, gently took him by the arms and propelled him towards the waiting moonhorse. "She's yours, Herbie. Say hello to her!"

Herbie stood in front of the moonhorse, feeling the light from her moonstone pass through him again and again. She lowered her head, her dark blue eyes, like crystals, seeming to grow so large as to enfold him; and he reached up to stroke her muzzle. At his touch, she neighed softly and struck one hoof on the roof, creating a shower of star-like sparks. Herbie kept his hand on her silver-white fur, for it gave him the most extraordinary feeling. Gone went his trembling, his awe, gone went the sense of himself as a boy caught up in a dark world of fog and cold: all he felt was love, love for this creature, for her silvery light, for the magnificence of her body and the beauty of her wings, and above all for the unqualified trust she had put in him. She made him feel more powerful than the moon and taller than the stars.

He could not bear to take his hands off her. Slowly, he worked his way around to her side. Her back seemed very high up, but the way he felt then made him think he could leap into the sky. He sprang up and was astride his moonhorse. She opened her wings and neighed again.

The other children clapped and whistled and called his name. It was a joyous moment for all of them.

They all knew what should happen now: Herbie would take his inaugural flight, just himself and the moonhorse alone in the dark sky above the fog, higher than he would ever fly with her again, so that they should get to know each other, bond into one. It was to be their most precious time of all. They watched him murmur something to her and gently nudge her flanks with his heels. She neighed again, but instead of taking flight, she struck her hind hoof once more.

"There's something wrong," said Herbie. "I can feel it."

He slid off the moonhorse and ran his eye over her anxiously. "It's like a little patch of shadow," he murmured, "in the light."

Will had slid down to perch on Keiron's shoe. *The back hoof, on the left,* Will said. *It's missing.*

"Herbie," Keiron called out. "She's lost a shoe."

Herbie lifted her leg. "It's true," he shouted in dismay.

"We have to find it," said Astar. "She won't fly properly without it."

"She'd get left behind," said Wag.

"She might not even make it to the Mooncastle," said Idé.

The sombre tones of their voices said it all.

"Spread out," said Jessie. "She may have dropped it on the roof."

They fanned out, searching. The further they got from the moonhorse, the more the fog encroached. The roofscape was vast, and they soon lost sight of each other and the moonhorse. Herbie stayed with her, unable to bear being apart from her for one second, full of anguish that she should suffer this loss.

Gradually, the children reassembled, empty-handed. They stood around, sad, wondering what else they could do.

All except Jessie and Keiron. They had teamed up on the far end of the roof where a lot of ivy reached to the parapet of the roof.

"I have a gift too, remember," Keiron said.

Using his telepathic ability to talk to inanimate objects, he had been asking brick and pipe, slate and trapdoor: *Have you seen any sign of the moonhorse's shoe?* As he neared the edge of the roof, he began to get hints of something. *We saw a ribbon of milky light cut down through the fog,* said an ornate chimney. *I heard a clink,* said a coping stone. *And I a rustle, as of something caught,* said the glass of a grimy window.

"It's somewhere here," he told Jessie. They peered over the battlements into the creeping, shadowy ivy, but could see nothing.

I'll go down, said Will. The little manikin shinned down a gnarled trunk and disappeared into the thick leaves. He climbed and slithered and leaped from branch to branch. A pigeon, roused from its sleep, pecked ferociously at him, and a snake hissed loudly, but he dodged out of the way. He knew how important this search was, not just for Herbie and the moon-horse, but for Keiron too.

And then he saw it. It had lodged in a large twig nest. A big black bird was perched on the nest above it, as if keeping guard. Will cursed. Birds, often mistaking him for a twig, had proved to be some of his worst enemies. How was he going to scare it away? He broke off some twigs and threw them at the bird, but they fell short or missed their target, and the bird merely ruffled its feathers angrily and squawked at him. He admitted defeat and climbed back up.

"I'm going down," said Keiron at once, and before Jessie could say anything, he was over the parapet, gripping the ivy, lowering himself down. Will guided him.

The bird flew off with a panicky flap of its glistening black wings as he approached. When he picked the horseshoe out of the nest, he felt something of what Herbie had felt on touching the moonhorse: a sense of happiness, light and love.

Well done, Will. What would I do without you?

Precious little, I expect, said Will with a happy laugh, clinging to the boy's hair.

Jessie cheered with relief when he saw the horse-shoe glowing in Keiron's hand. They leapt lightly, eagerly back to the moonhorse and held it up for everyone to see.

"Keiron found it," Jessie announced to the others. "He was led to it by a gift he has for talking to things in his head. Only *he* could have found it."

"Never mind about that," said Keiron. "Here, Herbie. I expect you know how to put it on."

Herbie took the horseshoe; his face was full of thanks, but he could not express it then. He raised his moonhorse's leg and placed the horseshoe in the right place. It fused immediately.

"That's extraordinary," said Keiron. "Did you know that was going to happen?"

Herbie nodded.

"Then I don't understand why it fell off."

There was a little silence after he said this. Cassie glanced at Astar, and then she said, "Keiron, I think they've been laying a little test for you."

"Test?" He looked from his sister to Jessie, and sort of understood. "Oh, is that fair?" he murmured, turning away, his eyes suddenly blurred with unexpected tears. Didn't they trust him?

He felt Jessie's arm on his shoulder. "I'm sorry, Keiron. We had to be sure. This is not just about friendship, you know. It's about much, much more. We all had to be absolutely sure that you were one of us. *Truly* one of us. You wouldn't have been able to find that horseshoe unless you were."

"Will found it, not me," Keiron muttered.

"Yes, but Will is part of you, isn't he?"

Keiron considered that. "Yes, I think he is," he said with conviction.

So do I, said Will.

"But still, I don't see..." Keiron began again.

"You will. Soon. You'll see why we had to be sure. You and your sister, together, are more important than any of us."

There was a swishing of wings and a stirring of breeze. They turned and saw Herbie on the back of his moonhorse. "Goodbye," he waved at them. "We're off at last." The horse rose into the circle of dark sky above them. They all waved furiously and happily until the fog crept back in and obscured the last traces of Herbie and his moonhorse sailing into the heavens.

CHAPTER 6

Cassie often found herself drawn to the windows in the sprawling and gloomy old building. It was partly because she yearned for the freedom of the outside world; partly because the endless, shifting masses of fog fascinated her in a gruesome sort of way. Shapes formed fleetingly, suggesting animals or fantastic creatures. Disembodied faces peered briefly at her, comic, grotesque or threatening. Others suggested landscapes of twilight snow... But what she was looking for – though she was barely conscious of doing so – was moonghosts. Until she had seen that one inside Numero – or thought she had – she had dismissed the idea of them. Now she wasn't so sure, and the very doubt niggled at her night and day.

One day, after lunch, she leaned out of a window. There was a brief break in the wall of fog, enough for her to see a barge paddling slowly across the lake.

She asked Astar about it.

"That'd be bringing the supplies. Food, and clothes, and that. It ferries them over every day."

"How do I get to it?" Cassie asked.

Astar laughed. "You'll never escape that way. It's

been tried too many times before. The crew are loyal, you can be sure of that."

"I realize that. I wasn't thinking of escape."

"What then?"

"I want to get a letter to my father."

"Oh, I see." Astar was thoughtful for a minute. "Well, you might succeed. But it will be risky. Groak doesn't like letters."

"Surprise, surprise," said Cassie ironically.

She smuggled pencil and paper into the dormitory that night and wrote a letter to Lord Tancred by candlelight. She told him how like a prison the place was; how she'd seen a brief nightmare vision of Prince Badrur staring down at her in bed; how they were as far as ever from finding the missing Golden Spur. "We're wasting our time here, Father," she concluded. "You must do your best to get us out." She was going to tell him about Herbie's moonhoorse, too, but Astar begged her not to, "In case it falls into the wrong hands." Cassie told him how much she and Keiron missed him, then folded the letter as securely as she could.

That was the easy bit.

Astar volunteered to go with her to the barge. They slipped out of their afternoon workshops, complaining of feeling unwell. Astar knew the way to the water tunnel where the supplies were unloaded. She leaned out of a window overlooking it and caught the attention of one of the crew, whom she knew from her Estate. "My father will reward you well," she promised him, "if you see that this letter is delivered to Lord Tancred." The young man took it surreptitiously, hoping they hadn't been seen.

But even as the girls were returning to the workshops, the letter was in the hands of the barge master and the young man was being chastised.

Before the afternoon was out, the letter was in Mr Groak's pudgy hands. Luckily, Cassie had not made any rude remarks about the him, otherwise he might have exploded there and then in a rage. He contented himself with a scowl and a curse and placed the letter carefully in a drawer, deciding to use it when the time suited him.

It was hard for the twins to get together alone for more than a few minutes each day, and they often ached for each other's company. They took to creeping by turns into each other's dormitory late at night to whisper their news to each other.

"I want to go back to the Magic workshop," Keiron said. "I didn't have time to see what was in it. Jessie is quite convinced it somehow belongs to us. I don't know why."

"Perhaps we'll find out," said Cassie, only too eager to join him.

They did not dare light a lamp until they were on the deserted workshop floor, and Will had to lead the way through the darkness. At the end of the dormitory corridor were the living quarters of some of the teachers, including Miss Rictus, and they feared she might be on one of her infrequent patrols.

The door to the Magic workshop opened at their touch. That struck them as rather mysterious, for several of the children in their class, alerted by Jessie, had tried to open it in the last few days and had found it locked; but Keiron, at least, was not surprised.

At first, the vast room appeared empty. There were dust and cobwebs everywhere. Nothing magical at all.

Gradually, they made out certain signs, patterns and lettering in the gloom. They soon realized that, oddly, the figure twelve predominated in the patterns around the wall. It was endlessly repeated as alternating figures and words in weird configurations. There were moons divided into twenty-four segments, like wheels with spokes. Painted on the ceiling were moonhorses, one larger than the others which surrounded it; the twins counted, without surprise, twelve in all.

On the floor they discovered, when they scuffed away the dust, the familiar picture of the Spurs, but with one difference. Around it was written a riddle: *For the Spurs, a two-headed rider, halved but one.*

"Don't get undressed," Jessie said to Keiron a few nights later. "It's the night of the full moon."

"What difference does that make?" Keiron asked, forgetting.

"All the difference in the world," Jessie grinned, teasingly. "Tonight, we shan't be going to bed. Tonight, you will get answers to all the questions you've been plaguing me with since you discovered your workshop."

As the thirteen children rose silently and descended stealthily to the chamber in the basement, the twins felt themselves curiously isolated from their classmates, not in an uncomfortable way, however, but with the feeling that a tremendous surprise awaited them. They followed the rest down two flights of stairs, feeling their way in the dark, terrified of slipping.

Luckily, Keiron had Will, who could see better in the dark, to guide him, and they reached the basement without mishap. They slid silently past the kitchens, down disused and damp passageways, and then down another narrow staircase to a door. One of the children had the key, and they all heard it turn in the lock.

I've been here before, Will declared excitedly. *It's where I saw. . .*

Ssh, Will, not now.

As soon as the door was closed, several lamps were lit. The light revealed the large circle in mosaic on the floor, divided into twelve segments, each labelled. The twins' eleven classmates stood in the segments corresponding to their own Estates. They joined hands and all looked at the twins.

"You can see that the circle is broken," said Jessie. "You will make it complete."

Astar nodded towards the twelfth segment. Its dust had been disturbed by Will earlier, partly revealing the mooncastle and the word *Magic*. "That is your Estate," she said. "The twelfth and most mysterious one. Take up your position there."

The twins stood on their segment and joined hands with the others. They were so awed by the solemnity of the occasion, they said nothing. They all stood in silence, savouring the sight of a complete circle: it was something the twins' classmates had often despaired of ever happening.

"Let us all sit," said Numero. They unlinked hands and sat cross-legged. The twins stared at the centre of the mosaic. It showed what looked like a brilliant, translucent, precious stone, radiating clear light into each of the segments. Surounding this, like a necklace, were eleven lesser lights, cloudy like moonstones. Only the twins' segment did not have one of these moonstones, and Cassie silently pointed this out to her brother.

"Now at last we are complete," said Numero. "We are twelve."

A murmur of satisfaction passed through the circle.

"Thirteen, surely?" Keiron interposed tentatively.

All eyes turned to him, some glowing mysteriously in the lamplight.

"You saw the riddle in the Magic workshop," said Jessie. "The Twelfth will be *a two-headed rider, halved but one.*"

The circle of children repeated this.

"We did not know what it meant," said Wag, shaking her head. "We thought it might be some strange, magical beast."

"We never guessed it would be twins," said Idé with a smile.

"You count as one," said Arturia, who came from the Estate of Art.

The twins glanced at one another: did they *feel* like one, they wondered.

There was a significant pause. Then Jessie said, as if by arrangement with the others, "You are the last of the Ancient Riders." He looked directly as Keiron. "I wanted to tell you this the other night, but I had to hold back until we were all absolutely sure."

"The last – and greatest – of the Ancient Riders has come," said Stave, who came from the Estate of Music. It was another signal, and all the children but the twins struck up a tuneful chant. They made out the words:

> *"For each of the moonhorses*
> *an Ancient Rider,*
> *riding the Estates and the city, wider.*
> *The last to come by the rule of twelve*
> *halved like the Spurs, in magic delve. . ."*

When the chant was finished, Keiron said, "Tell us what an Ancient Rider is."

Jessie spoke for them. "Many, many years ago, the first and greatest moonhorse was born. He was made by the Goddess of the Moon, of some bright and airy substance. In his forehead was placed a magical diamond, and he was given a Mooncastle here on this island to live in."

"Then the great fog came," said Herbie, taking up the story. "The Diamond Horse found he could clear it away on his own by the flapping of his wings, but only on the night when the moon is at its strongest, and only around the Mooncastle."

"To clear the fog over the whole island, he needed eleven other moonhorses, making the circle of twelve," said Structus, who came from the Estate of Technology. "Their combined power alone can do it."

"So every one hundred and forty-four years, a new moonhorse was born on the moon and sent here." Arturia said, taking up the story. "And the circle of light in the fog grew wider."

"Each time, a new Estate was formed to look after the new-born moonhorse," said Wag.

"And each moonhorse needed a rider," Numero added.

"When we become twelve, the moonhorses are passed on to us. You saw that with Herbie," said Idé.

"And when each of *our* first children become twelve," said Herbie, "they will take over as the moonhorses' riders."

"This is the first time in the history of the moon-horses that there have been eleven Children of the Estates, all aged twelve at once," Astar explained. "We call ourselves the Ancient Riders, for there have been Riders ever since the first moonhorse."

There was a silence.

"There's something you haven't told us," Cassie said tentatively. "Who is the Diamond Horse's rider?"

The Ancient Riders glanced at each other significantly.

"We think you two are," said Astar. "The riddle points to you: *halved but one*."

This was such an extraordinary idea, the twins could barely grasp it. They leaned against each other, thinking "Us? The Rider of the Diamond Horse?" Surely their coming here had not been prophesied for so long?

Seeking to make sense of all this, Keiron said, "But you all come from Estates. We don't. We're foreigners."

"That is simply answered," said Jessie. "We think your Estate is the Mooncastle. The first one and the finest."

"Then tell us about the Mooncastle," Cassie asked, trying to understand this latest revelation.

"That is not easy," said Arturia. "Mix moonlight and fog, sculpt it into fantastic towers, add streams of light and flickering translucent walls, then watch it all form as the fog clears. We've never been in it, we've only seen it on the hill."

"It's your Estate," said Jessie. "I expect you must be the first to go in it."

The twins felt almost overwhelmed by these ideas. They listened in trembling excitement as the children described the Diamond Horse and the awe they felt in his presence.

Eventually, they all fell silent. There was a tense feeling of expectancy in the air.

"What happens now?" Keiron asked.

Jessie held up his hand. "Listen," he whispered. They heard the clock boom midnight. "Come, it is time."

The circle broke up. The children climbed stealthily to the roof of the building, taking care not to rouse Miss Rictus or any of the other staff. This night of all nights they had to be sure that they were not disturbed, for what they were about to do that night, as on every night of the full moon, was known only to the Councillors, their families and their most trusted staff. A few of the longer-serving and more civilized of the school staff knew too, and they had agreed among themselves that Mr Groak and Miss Rictus should not be told in case they tried to interfere.

On the roof, an incredible and beautiful sight met the children. Side by side in a long row, their wings half-open, their heads turned, stood the island's eleven white moonhorses. They were waiting for their riders. The whole roof glowed with the light of their moonstones.

The Ancient Riders ran to their moonhorses, stroked and fondled them, talked to them in their own private language; then they mounted them.

The twins were left standing, at a loss. Where was the Diamond Horse? If they were his rider, surely he should be here?

"Can't we ride with you?" Keiron asked Jessie.

"Not tonight," said Jessie, shaking his head. "The horses wouldn't allow it."

"But I thought ... I mean, when will the Diamond Horse come for us?"

All the Ancient Riders paused when they heard that and looked at Cassie a little pityingly.

"We've never known the Diamond Horse to leave the Mooncastle," Stave explained. "He's waiting for you to come to him."

"We think only something incredible, extraordinary, would make him leave the Mooncastle," said Arturia. "We don't know why."

"It's like he's saving himself," said Jessie, grasping for an idea that was only half-formed.

"You must be patient. Your time will soon come," said Astar. "Go back to the dormitory. We'll see you tomorrow morning before we all leave for our estates."

One by one the moonhorses rose into the foggy night. Each one became a blur of light, then gradually faded into the fog.

The twins watched until the last trace of the moonhorses had disappeared. The fog closed around them and they shivered.

"I wish we were flying with them," said Cassie wistfully.

"I don't see how we can get to the Mooncastle if they won't let us ride their moonhorses," Keiron said, a touch resentful.

"This place is full of rules, isn't it. The rule of law. The rule of twelve... They don't do things just because they might want to." She sighed.

"Come on, it's cold out here," said Keiron. "I'll come to your dormitory, if you like. I don't fancy spending the rest of the night on my own."

But, at the entrance to the stairs, Keiron paused and rummaged frantically in his pockets and his hair. He was in for a little shock: Will was no longer with him. He ran his hands over his clothes, calling Will's name. Thinking back, he had a vague recollection of Will murmuring something and then shinning down his leg.

They blundered about in the fog looking for him, calling for him, but with no success. Keiron soon became convinced that Will, on a sudden, unprecedented impulse, had gone with the Ancient Riders.

CHAPTER 7

The twins woke late the following morning with a sense that while they had slept their world had changed. At first, they became conscious of the noise of many people moving about and talking. Usually, the school was full of restrained silence, quiet footsteps, whispers. Not this morning. The whole building sounded as if it was on the move. Voices rose; there was chatter, shrieks and laughter. It was as if they had been partially deaf when inside the school, hearing everything muffled, from a distance; the noise was quite a shock.

Rising, they got an even greater surprise. Light flooded through the dormitory windows. Peering out, they gasped. *No fog!* The island was clear of fog! They could see right over the lake to the landscape of trees beyond, with the towers of the city just visible in the distance. And a weak sun shone down on everything, making the colours of the lake and the trees seem extraordinarily vivid, as if a gauze had been lifted from the scene.

"Fogless Day!" Keiron declared. "That's when everyone in school goes home for the day, isn't it?"

"Do you think we'll be allowed to go, too?" Cassie asked eagerly. "Will Father be waiting for us on the shore?"

"Oh, I do hope so," said Keiron. "Then perhaps we can get away from here for good."

The door burst open and the girls from their class streamed in. They looked bright and happy and were laughing and chatting in a way the twins had not seen before. Several of them briefly hugged Cassie or ruffled Keiron's hair, but they seemed too excited at their imminent release to stop and talk to them.

Jessie came in behind them.

"Did Will go with you last night?" Keiron asked him. "We can't find him."

Jessie grinned. "Yes, I felt him wriggling up my back and into my hair after we had taken off. Didn't you know?"

Keiron grinned with relief and shook his head. "Oh, I hope you didn't mind?"

"He kept out of sight. Here," and he fished the abashed-looking manikin from his pocket. "I'll leave you to tell him off."

I only did it for you, Will protested a little sheepishly. *I'll talk to you later.*

Yes, and if you don't shout at me too much, I might tell you about the amazing things I saw. Or, there again, I might not!

"Is your father meeting you?" Jessie asked.

"We hope so," said Cassie.

"Well, if you want, you could stay in our town house again."

"Will you be there?" asked Keiron.

"No, I'm flying back to the Estate on my moonhorse. I'm sorry, there won't be time for you to come with me. Fogless Day only lasts for twenty-four hours."

"We'll see you back here, then," said Astar.

The twins exchanged glances. Not if they could help it, they thought.

Astar saw the glance. "Don't think of trying to escape," she said. "They'll hunt you down soon enough, and then you'll be put in the Dark Room as a punishment. Please."

"We'll see what Father says," Keiron said.

A great gong boomed through the building, signalling it was time to leave. Quickly, the children hugged the twins and said their farewells.

"We usually fly back to our Estates at night," said Wag, hurrying towards the door. "But everything was delayed because of Herbie."

"We shall be seen," said Idé.

"It can't be helped," said Astar.

"Well, it won't do the children and their parents harm to see the moonhorses once in a while," said Jessie, looking on the bright side. "Let's just hope Groak and Rictus don't guess what's happening."

The moonhorses were waiting on the roof. The twins watched them take off one by one into the clear blue sky; they waved until the last moonhorse was out of sight.

"Isn't the sun beautiful," Cassie sighed.

"Everything is so bright," said Keiron, shielding his eyes. He leaned over the battlements. "Look, the first boats are leaving."

They watched the children being ferried across the

lake. On the opposite bank were a crowd of parents, eagerly waiting to pick up their children.

"I hope Father is down there," said Cassie, scanning the crowd with narrowed eyes. She was longing to see him. "Come on, let's go and look."

They turned to leave – and there was Miss Rictus, squinting and ugly, at the top of the stairs. "There you are," she said, out of breath, a sour look on her face. "What on earth are you doing up here? You know the roof is out-of-bounds."

She leaned against a chimney stack to get her breath. How yellow and withered she looks, thought Cassie. "The Headmaster wishes to see you at once. In his study. Now come on, you've kept him waiting long enough, and he's not in a good mood."

"But..." said Keiron, his mouth dropping open in disbelief.

"We're about to go ashore," Cassie explained.

"Are you?" Miss Rictus said with a pitiless smile. "Not before you've seen Mr Groak."

She followed behind them. Halfway down the stairs, Keiron whispered, "We could make a run for it." But when they turned a corner in the stairs they came across Mr Groak himself.

"Get to my study immediately," he bellowed at them, his sidewhiskers trembling.

Sandwiched between the two people they feared and hated most in the school, they felt cowed. Miss Rictus pushed them forward along the corridor to the headmaster's study.

Mr Groak lowered himself on to a tall, black chair behind his desk and glared at them. His whiskers quivered angrily. "It is a privilege to go ashore on Fogless Day," he announced. "In return for obedient behaviour and sustained effort. You two have, according to Miss Rictus, applied yourself to the work, which rather surprises me, I must say. But on the matter of obedience..."

"We've not done anything wrong," Keiron protested.

"You, I recall, behaved abysmally on your first night here, boy. And as for your sister..."

"What about me?" Cassie challenged.

With a triumphant little grin, and a glance at Miss Rictus, Mr Groak removed from a drawer in his desk the letter Cassie had written to her father. "Do you recognize this?" he said, tossing it contemptuously in front of her.

Cassie went white, first with dismay, then with anger.

"Trying to smuggle out subversive messages is an offence against the Precepts."

"How dare you!" Cassie spluttered.

Mr Groak's face darkened. "If you are trying to challenge my authority in this..." he threatened.

"Of course she's not," Keiron butted in, laying a restraining hand on his sister. He saw the prospect of their leaving the school crumbling before his eyes, but something might be salvaged from it. "She was only writing to our father. We miss him."

Mr Groak waved a dismissive hand at him. "Transgress, and you will be punished. You should have learnt that by now."

But Cassie's nerve had been touched at its most sensitive point. She was furious, and that, rising like a red mist before her eyes, blinded her to consequences. She suddenly appeared to lose control. She pounded her fists on the desk, shrieking through her teeth; and then, as Miss Rictus tried to grab her from behind, she pushed the old woman away, turned back to the desk and with one magnificent gesture, swept all of Mr Groak's belongings on to the floor. Then she stood with her hands on her hips and shouted such abuse at the headmaster, that he stood for a moment paralysed in amazement: never had he ever been spoken to like this, least of all by a pupil.

For her pains, Cassie was slung in the Dark Room.

Keiron protested so much, he was thrown in after her.

They sat in a dank, dripping room, in dense darkness, somewhere down in the basement.

"That was magnificent," said Keiron.

"Yes, but this isn't, is it."

"Well, it was worth it, just to see the look on old Groak's face. I wish I'd have said those things. Magnificent!"

She squeezed her brother's arm gratefully: he always knew when to say the right things. "Yes, but what about Father?"

Fog provides ideal cover for those who want anonymity, or to slip away unseen. Lord Tancred was determined that he would be on the bank with the other parents on Fogless Day, to be reunited with their children. Days before, he had slipped away from the Estate of Music where he had been storytelling, and he had found his way to the school more by luck than judgement, and just in time.

But now, as the last of the children were ferried over from the school, he was disturbed and angry that there was no sign of the twins.

None of the ferries were returning to the school. It took him some time to find a boat, and it was mid-morning before he alighted on the island. But a terrible frustration awaited him there. All the doors to the school were locked and silent in response to his repeated knocking. He shouted up at windows. With everyone but Mr Groak and Miss Rictus away on the mainland, the place seemed deserted.

Eventually, the Headmaster did hear him. Leaning out of a window, he merely said, "You're wasting your time. Your children have broken the most basic Precept of obedience and are being punished. Come back next Fogless Day; maybe they will have learnt their lesson by then." His head disappeared inside the window before Tancred could protest.

Never had he felt so helpless. The doors were barred against him, the windows on the ground floor mere slits; and with no means of climbing the sheer walls, it was hopeless. He decided his only hope was to petition the Council for their release. It was barbaric that he and his children should be treated like this.

He looked across the glinting metallic water, now dazzling in the light, and thought of the goddess Citatha. Why did she always have to put them through so many trials in order to find the missing pieces of the Golden Armour?

Come on, then, Will, said Keiron, *tell us what happened to you last night.*

Ah, well, it happened like this, Will answered with satisfaction. *I clung to Jessie's hair. I couldn't see much because of the fog, but I knew we were flying over vast stretches of dark forest.*

After each sentence or so, he paused to allow Keiron to repeat it to Cassie, giving him time to get the sequence and the detail just right.

Then there was a soft disc of light ahead; it got bigger and bigger until the fog gave way. We hovered over the rim of an old volcano, and as the fog cleared, I saw that in the middle of it was this amazing castle. It seemed to be made of light and mist, because you could see the walls shifting like mist in a bottle; it was all silvery light, tall towers, battlements that glittered like stars in the moonlight. Beautiful!

Will sighed. Keiron had to urge him to go on.

We landed in front of the castle and formed a circle, facing inwards.

The drawbridge lowered and out came the finest horse I have ever seen. It was the colour of the moon, but brighter and purer, larger than the others, and very proud. I had to shield my eyes for a while.

"The Diamond Horse?" Cassie asked, after Keiron had relayed Will's words to her.

Will nodded.

He stood in the centre of our circle and held up the great diamond in his forehead to the light of the moon. The diamond caught the moonlight and seemed to gather it: the gem glowed brighter and brighter. Then, with the light almost blinding us, he turned to each moonhorse and beamed some of that light right into their moonstones. You could see it travelling between them, and the moonstones glowed much brighter than I've ever seen before.

"That must have been an amazing sight," Keiron interrupted, feeling a pang of jealousy that he had not seen it for himself.

Then the Diamond Horse joined the circle. He was the only one without a rider, and it struck me as so odd.

Anyway, all the horses turned outwards and flapped their wings, not haphazardly, but in slow motion and all in unison, like a dance. I had to cling fast to Jessie's moonhorse, and a good job I did, for I would have been blown away. A great wind uncoiled from the centre of the circle and spread out. It tore the fog around the castle into shreds and blew it away. It blew and blew, growing wider and wider, shredding the fog.

"Fogless Day!" Cassie exclaimed. "That's how it happens."

Well, at last, when the night was clear of fog and the moon had sunk to the treetops, the Diamond Horse said farewell to each of the moonhorses and returned to his castle. I felt sorry for him walking away alone like that.

The moonhorses took off. The whole island stretched around us on that return journey, the dawn coming up, the last wisps of the fog being blown away. Flying is a wonderful feeling; I love it.

"But why is the fog only cleared for twenty-four hours?" Keiron said a little later.

He hasn't got a rider, said Will. *All the other moonhorses have except him. And when he returned to the castle, he had no one waiting for him.*

"He's waiting for us," said Cassie. "We are his Ancient Rider."

"You mean, he needs us before he can clear the fog for good?"

Cassie shrugged. "I think so. But I don't quite see what part the Spurs play in all this, do you?"

"No, but they must, somehow."

"We must get to the Diamond Horse somehow."

But sitting in the dark of the punishment cell, alone and hungry, that seemed a remote and forlorn prospect.

CHAPTER 8

Badrur still had his ship's compass. Throughout his tough, interminable journey through vast tracts of inhospitable forest, its little needle, pointing out his path, probably saved his life. Many a hunter or trapper, wandering in the fog from the forest paths, had died from thirst or starvation, driven mad by the monotony of trees.

The conviction that he was the Dark Rider had grown upon him. His mind was inflamed with visions of himself on a great, black, flying stallion, casting terror and death around him. He saw himself slash a path through a throng of guards in the Sanctuary and snatch the left Golden Spur, to wear it on his exalted heel. He saw himself descend on the School, impale the odious Groak and his henchwoman Rictus, and abduct the twins. They would lead him to the right Golden Spur. With the power of the Horse of the Eclipse, combined with that of the Spurs, who could then stand against him? It would match even the power of the goddess Citatha, he told himself, and his black heart nearly burst at the thought of the duels they would surely fight for ultimate supremacy.

On the north-eastern coast of the the island rose the Tower of the Eclipse. It was tall and monumental, made of some black stone or slate, rising sheer above the trees. Who had built it or why no one knew, although many a story had been spun to account for its existence. Shrouded in fog for most of its time, and known through legends than actual sightings, it loomed large and fearful in the minds of the islanders. On its conical roof flew a stone horse in petrified flight, on its back a rider all in black, his cloak billowing out.

Not far from the coast drifted a ship. It had only one crew member – a giant of a child. She was sun-burnt and wind-whipped by weeks at sea. Hearing the waves on the shore, her dark, unfathomable eyes flicked open.

She saw the tower and sat up. It was the first sign of life she had seen along the coast for days and there was something about it which attracted her. Besides, she was hungry and thirsty and yearned to walk free on land again.

But what of Prince Badrur? She had followed him here from East Island, and had lost him somewhere along the featureless coast. She did not for a moment imagine that he had been drowned; no, this was where he must have landed.

She jumped into the water and swam towards the shore. The sea was quite calm here and the fog that had hung about the coast had miraculously cleared that morning. Presently, she realized she wasn't alone in the water. There were large, sleek, silver-blue creatures swimming with her. She was so delighted, she stopped swimming and they stopped too. They circled her, making friendly high-pitched squeaks, peering at her through small, bright eyes. She stopped splashing, held herself still, put out her hand and coaxed a few of them nearer. They allowed her to stroke their smooth, oily skins, and they showed pleasure at her touch by turning this way and that, squeaking excitedly.

The Child, since her strange birth on North Island, brought back from the dead by Cassie's healing hands, had never known any friends. She had discovered early on that a touch of her hand, with the merest intention to harm, proved fatal to any creature that came near her. She had grown large on their death, for somehow, at the point of death, she absorbed their life spirit, and grew in size and strength.

None of this she had understood; the destruction she had caused was blind. But, as these sleek and friendly creatures swam around her, obviously delighting in her company, she became aware that she must not touch them in that way. She must like them, play with them, not get angry with them. Then they wouldn't grow limp and still and be no more use to her. It was a new thought to her, and it burst into her mind as bright as the sunshine on the water.

She was consciously gentle with them; but the change this represented inside her made her feel awkward, self-conscious; so that, in a sudden panic, she struck out for the coast. The creatures swam either side of her, silent now, curving out of the water, then disappearing.

She sat on the coast. They bobbed up and down in the water for a while, watching her; then they took off, and she watched them skimming away, until they blurred into nothingness.

She felt lonely and cried a bit. Then, remembering her hunger and thirst, she clambered inland.

At the foot of the Tower of the Eclipse was a rockpool of water. She lapped from it for some time, until her thirst was quenched, then she washed the sea-salt and grime from her body. In the forest, she found leaves and fruit of a sort she could just about eat.

Then she pushed open the door of the tower and climbed the spiral staircase to the first floor. It was bare. Here the sound of the sea was muffled and the sun shone through the slits in the stone. She settled down, thankful to be on a surface that did not sway with the waves, and promptly fell asleep.

She woke the next morning to a world of fog. It shifted about the tower, forming fleeting shapes, of ghosts and masks and fantastic beasts, and watching that ghostly panorama kept her amused for hours.

Eventually, she tired of that. It was time to set off inland.

There were no hunters' paths here. As she pushed her way slowly through the trees, she kept looking back at the tower. It appeared fleetingly in the wind-blown fog at first; it was the only landmark she knew and she was curiously reluctant to lose sight of it.

She trekked on slowly. And then she had an accident. Her foot slid into a concealed hole in the rocky earth. She howled with pain. She had twisted her ankle. She hopped about, angry and amazed; she was not used to pain, nor the sense of vulnerability it brought with it. She stared at her red and swollen ankle in hurt puzzlement.

As soon as grey light crept through the trees, she began the painful, hobbling journey back to the tower. She wanted to lick her wounds there.

It took a week for the deep pain to ease away.

As soon as she could walk comfortably again, she thought of her friends the sea creatures. She was overjoyed to find them swimming about just off the coast. She plunged into the water and played with them until nightfall. They were her first thought the next day, too, and for days after; they seemed as delighted by her company as she was with theirs.

But one day the Child got over-excited in a game of water-catch. She lunged out too hard at one of the creatures in an attempt to reach it, and stunned it. The rest of the creatures surrounded the inert, silently floating body, nudged it with their noses, squeaked at it. Then they turned on the Child and shrieked their shock, their anger, their pain at her, a noise and a hostility she could hardly bear. She felt they were all turning against her.

She carried the creature back to the shore. There, she laid it on the sand, stroked it, crooned to it, willing it to come alive.

Suddenly, it opened its eyes and twitched violently.

The Child sprang back, then cried out with relief. She had the sense to see that the creature was struggling for its life on the sand. With some difficulty, for it would not stop wriggling, she scooped it up and carried it back to the sea. Twice on the way it flew out of her hands.

As soon as it was in the water, the creature slid rapidly away from her. It swum out thankfully to its family. Together, the creatures, which she had come to love so much, disappeared into the foggy sea, without one last look at her.

The Child sat on the sand, feeling sorry for herself. But she wasn't as despondent as she might have been. She was pleased she had saved the life of the creature; it was a new feeling for her, and she liked it.

She woke on the beach. Night had stolen in. Looking back towards the tower, she thought she saw a flickering light.

Outside the tower, a horse was tethered. It reared up and neighed in fright when it saw her. The noise brought a head to the window. Looking up, she saw to her joy that it was he who she had been looking for. Prince Badrur.

At the school, the twins were having a grindingly hard and monotonous time.

They had been kept in the Dark Room without food or water until the rest of the children returned at the end of Fogless Day. They were told that their father had been waiting for them on the shore, and that made them more bitter. Somehow, they would find a way of escape; another twenty-four days of this seemed intolerable.

In the mornings, as usual, they were set to learn the Precept for the month, which, at the spin of the Spur wheel in the Sanctuary, was Fear – fear of authority, of parents, of doing wrong, of punishment, of moonghosts; fear, above all, of the Horse of the Eclipse. In the afternoon they turned out useless little metal spurs which the teachers delighted in criticizing for some often imagined defect.

But mercifully, the pattern of their lives at the school at last began to break up. It began a week before the next Fogless Day.

One night Cassie was woken by Astar shaking her shoulder.

"Cassie, you've got to come with me at once." There was panic in her voice, and Cassie sat up, alert. Of all the children in her class, she considered Astar the most fearless; yet now the girl was trembling.

"What's the matter?"

"Just come with me. Hurry."

She pulled on some clothes and flitted behind Astar up to the roof. There she was surprised to see Astar's moonhorse. What was it doing here?

"She's flown in from our city house," said Astar. "There was a note tied around her neck. It says my mother is very ill. The moonghosts have invaded her and she's coughing her life away. She was bad when I was home last, and I told her about how you cured Numero of his cough. Now she's worse and my father thinks she will die soon. Will you come to her?"

With no more than a nod, Cassie climbed on to the back of the moonhorse behind her friend. "I thought you only rode your moonhorse on Fogclear Night," she said, thinking what an easy escape route this would have been.

"We do. But this is an emergency. She would only break the rule for this."

The moonhorse's wings flapped, the fog around them cleared, and they took off. Nothing could be seen beyond the edge of the fog, but Cassie found the swish of the great wings, the movement of the air around her, the sense of freedom, exhilarating.

They landed on the roof of Astar's town house, between two gables.

Cassie could hear Astar's mother coughing the minute she stepped into the house. Astar led the way to her bedside. In the lamplight, she was pale and sweating, her face convulsed with pain each time she coughed.

"Helyna," her husband said, leaning over his wife, his face anxious and drawn. "Astar is here with her friend."

Cassie laid her hands on the woman's chest. She sensed at once that the disease was more rampant than Numero's had been, that the lungs were all but covered with dark and shifting shadows. She willed her healing energy into the woman's body. It flowed around the shadows, like light attacking fog, and for what seemed an interminable time there seemed to be a battle of equal forces.

Helyna arched in pain, and let out a long, thin moan.

Cassie saw the shadows in her lungs flicker and shift, thin and dissolve.

Slowly, Helyna's body subsided, the moan petered out. Those who stood around the bed – for several of the household had joined them by then – heard her sigh, in profound relief.

But it was not quite over. Then, as before, but clearer this time, Cassie saw a moonghost inside her patient. Its hollow eyes were dark and malevolent, and a silent hiss of pure hate seemed to issue from its dark mouth. It loomed larger and larger in Cassie's mind. She watched it, helpless, as it reached out to her with blurred grey fingers. And only when it was within a few inches of her did it recoil suddenly, as if scalded.

Cassie let go of Helyna with a little scream.

She shuddered uncontrollably. It was as if she had been touched with something evil herself. She felt tainted by it. There is no doubting the existence of the moonghosts now, she thought.

The thanks and praise she received from the family, and most of all from Helyna, for the "miraculous cure" hardly touched her. "I feel terribly tired," she said. "May I sleep here?"

Astar knew that they should return to the school before they were missed. But her friend looked exhausted. She showed her to a bed.

Cassie held up the golden spur pendant that Jessie's mother had given her. "I think I was saved from the moonghost by this," she murmured.

"I wonder why this spur works, and not any of the ones we make," Astar murmured, turning it in her hand.

Cassie woke to the sound of a throng outside. Opening the window, she saw that a small crowd had gathered below. Seeing her, they pointed, and called.

"Please come down. My husband is sick. You must come and see him."

"My little girl won't last much longer. Please help her."

Astar leaned out of the window beside her. "Somehow, word got out last night about my mother's cure. You're the miracle-worker now. But we haven't really got much time..."

"Oh, I must go to them. I can't let them suffer."

"The city is full of people with lung disease. You couldn't possibly..."

"I must."

Cassie hurried from house to house that morning, urged on by anxious relatives of the ill and the dying. She laid her hands on many painful chests, pouring her healing energy over dark shadows, sensing the evil moonghost writhing inside each body. She came away from each patient with the sound of tears and thanks ringing in her ears, and with a sensation of profound fear growing in her soul. A whole legion of moonghosts had fastened themselves on the people and were turning the living into the dead: she had but caught a glimpse of this, but it shook her to her roots.

By midday she was too exhausted to heal anyone else; even so, Astar had to push her forcibly up the stairs towards the moonhorse and help her mount.

The moonhorse took off and flew them back through the fog to the school. They alighted on the roof and waved goodbye to the moonhorse.

"I shall see him again next week," Astar said. "On Fogclear Night. Perhaps you will meet your father then."

"Oh, I do hope so," Cassie yawned, her eyelids heavy. All she wanted to do was sleep.

But they had not reckoned on the reception that awaited them. The minute they appeared in the workshops, hoping vainly that they had not been missed, they were sent to Miss Rictus. She harangued them furiously for an hour, trying without success to find out where they had been. Eventually, to appease her, they made up some story about exploring the unused parts of the great building and losing track of time. She threw them into a punishment cell.

Badrur saw the Child advancing out of the swirling fog towards the tower, and his heart sank in utter dismay. There was no creature he disliked more than this over-sized infant. She had dogged his footsteps since their fateful first encounter – when he had looked into her eyes and seen not the innocent soul he was expecting, but vast, cold, cosmic spaces. It was at that moment that she had conceived a hideous attachment to him which he could not break. On North Island, she had unthinkingly thwarted a battle between his forces and the forces of Lord Tancred, just as he was nearing victory. On East Island, she had playfully stopped up the Sacred Spring that alone gave power to his mother the Queen, creating the rebellion that led to her downfall. And now, here she was again!

He would have killed her long ago; but there was an invisible protective barrier around her which, as far as he knew, nothing could penetrate, neither monsters nor missiles. He was deeply envious of that barrier – what would he have given to possess it himself.

He ran swiftly down the stairs and locked the tower door. Then from a window, he swore, ground his teeth, hurled insults at her; but it was all water off a duck's back to her, she just clapped her hands and from time to time shrieked her happiness that she had found him again.

He withdrew, sat on the floor and waited. Soon weariness overtook him and he fell asleep. He had no idea that when he awoke, his whole life would change. For him this was to be no ordinary night.

The Child settled in a hollow in the ground, content that he was nearby, and watched shapes in the fog shift and reform. Night fell, and she dozed.

When she roused herself, feeling hungry, she woke to a world clear of fog and bathed in bright moonlight. The change was so startling, she had the sensation that she had woken in another place – but no, there was the tower, and there was the prince, leaning out of the window and staring at the big round moon. She stared at it too. It was like a wide and brilliant eye in the sky, watching them both.

As she watched something began to invade its edge. A crescent of blackness that gradually grew larger, like an eyelid slowly closing. Something huge and round was moving slowly and inexorably across the moon, blotting out the light. The Child stood up and murmured in growing distress.

Badrur watched the silver light dim and the world grow gradually darker and darker. He felt exhilarated by the slow darkening of the moonlit world. This was undoubtedly an eclipse – but was it *the* eclipse, the one prophesied, when the Horse of the Eclipse would ride the dark looking for its rider?

The crescent became a circle, the eclipse became complete. The corona of moonlight around the dark and solid disc made everything eerie, and there was an extraordinary silence, as if the world was holding its breath.

Badrur felt his nerves tighten and tighten. Something momentous was about to happen – *and happen to him.*

Out of the heart of the eclipse's darkness a shape formed. A being. It projected into space, then broke away. Nothing could be seen of it from the island for quite some time, but Badrur sensed its coming. It flapped great black wings. Riding the currents of the night air, it swept the heavens with its jet-black eyes, and fixed its sights on the Tower of the Eclipse. That was its destination. That, and the prince who stood in it.

Badrur saw it as a speck at first. He strained his eyes. Never had his heart beaten so fast.

A flying horse! This was it. The Horse of the Eclipse. Looking for his Dark Rider. He skimmmed through the scudding clouds, growing larger and larger.

Hovering with great black wings, he landed on a rock jutting out to sea, in direct view of the tower. The moon was just begining to emerge from its eclipse, and the eerie light slowly revealed the magnificence of the beast.

Badrur stared at him with trembling awe. For once in his life he felt dwarfed by a greater being.

His eyes were drawn to a stone set in his forehead, like a glittering black gem. It sent out a beam of darkness that sought out the prince. He felt it pass over him, probing him; he shuddered through and through, as if, under the scrutiny of that dark stone, every fibre of his being was undergoing a fundamental challenge.

Then he felt a powerful impulse to approach the beast, one which he could not deny even if he had wanted to. He hurried down the stairs, unlocked the tower door, and raced out.

The startled Child tried to reach out to him, but he dodged her and ran almost frantically towards the Horse, suddenly fearful that it might elude him. He stumbled and slithered on the wet rock in his haste until he was standing in front of the beast.

The Horse of the Eclipse spread his great wings. Badrur, with extraordinary energy, took one enormous leap and landed on its back. He felt the Horse shiver just once, and then a powerful force, like a wave of darkness, passed through him. It exhilarated him so much he threw his hands in the air, lifted his head and shouted in triumph. He was the Dark Rider. Together, he and this magnificent beast, child of the moon's eclipse, would ride the island, scattering death, disease and destruction.

The Horse's wings flapped and the beast rose a little. He moved slowly inland.

Below, the Child was beside herself with fear at the prince's escape. As the Horse of the Eclipse passed overhead, she took a superhuman leap upwards. She just managed to grasp hold of the beast's left rear ankle. The Horse dipped and bellowed and kicked furiously with its other rear foot, but the Child hung on grimly. She had enormous strength herself, and a density, a darkness inside her which was a match for the beast. Badrur tried to lean down and slash at her hand with a knife, but her barrier of protection deflected it.

The Horse of the Eclipse neighed in anger and struggled furiously, but he could not shake her off, not then; he would have to wait until the Child got tired. He had no choice but to rise into the night with her hanging on to his ankle, carrying both passengers towards the city.

CHAPTER 9

As usual on Fogclear Night, the Ancient Riders gathered in the hidden chamber. They felt subdued and nervous, although they could not say why. They all knew that the eclipse could occur at any time, but, like everyone in the school and in the city, they did not know it was to be that night. Perhaps the feeling of uneasy expectancy they felt was linked to the twins. Was it tonight that they were to be taken to the Mooncastle to meet the Diamond Horse?

"Can we only go on Fogclear Night?" Keiron wondered. "I mean, perhaps one of your moonhorses would take us there another day?"

The suggestion did not meet with approval. "None of us ever see the Diamond Horse except on Fogclear Night," Arturia explained patiently. "We do not know why, but it must be the same for you."

"Then perhaps we have to make our own way there," said Cassie. She knew the trip through the forest would be difficult, but anything was preferable to another month or more in the school.

But the Ancient Riders found that almost amusing. "No one gets through that forest," they smiled. "How else do you think the Diamond Horse has remained untouched all this while?"

The twins shrugged.

Ritual words were spoken, in counterpoint and unison, and the chant was sung again. There was some apprehensive talk of the Horse of the Eclipse. And then silence. The twins had never seen them in this strange, tense mood before.

Eventually, Idé said, "The moonhorses must be on the roof by now. We can't delay any longer."

The Ancient Riders rose and made their way quietly up through dark and twisting stairways to the roof. They were curiously relieved to see the row of moonhorses waiting there. But something was wrong. The moonhorses were twitching apprehensively, snorting nervously, pawing the roof. Worse, the light in their moonstones was flickering; it had lost its gentle, persistent glow. This more than anything upset the Ancient Riders, and they whispered together for some time, trying to find a reason for it.

They're scared, said Will. *That's all there is to it.*

They get their light and strength from the moon, don't they? Keiron replied. *So it must be something to do with that.*

And what threatens moonlight? Will prompted.

The eclipse! Are you saying. . .? Then it must be tonight!

He whispered the idea to Cassie. She shivered. "Don't tell them," she whispered back. "They're upset enough as it is."

The Ancient Riders mounted their moonhorses.

Shall I go with them again? Will asked.

If you like. I'll ask Jessie to take you.

Jessie gladly tucked Will into his pocket.

Cassie found herself fingering the golden spur pendant on her neck. Impulsively, she unclasped it and held it out to Astar. "Take this," she said, "in case you need protection." Astar took it gratefully; but those within earshot were left uneasy at Cassie's words.

"Here, take mine too," said Keiron to Jessie.

"But I shan't need that," Jessie protested mildly.

Keiron shrugged. "You never know. It can't do you any harm."

"But I gave it to you, for your protection."

"I'm only lending it."

Jessie took it and placed it round his neck. He smiled, and Keiron knew that he had been right to insist.

The moonhorses rose one by one. Their wings dispersed much of the fog around them. The twins watched them enviously until the fog closed in again, cold and clammy.

"Oh, I wish we were going with them," Cassie sighed, more than ever vexed at being left behind again. "If we're meant to be the rider of the Diamond Horse, why doesn't he come and get us? Or send some creature to take us there?"

"I don't know. I wonder if the Diamond Horse has ever left his Mooncastle, though? It's as if he doesn't want to without his rider."

"Then how do we get to him?" Cassie almost wailed. "Why is everything so complicated?

"Father always says magic has its own rules..."

"...which aren't always logical. Yes, I know."

"Well, Will'll tell us what happens. I expect it'll be just the same as last time. Except he *thinks* there might be an eclipse of the moon tonight. I wonder if he's right."

Flying a moonhorse was not just an exhilarating experience, it had the effect of cleansing spirits too; the Ancient Riders would end their flight feeling renewed and wiser. But they sensed at once that on this Fogclear Night it would not be the same. The moonhorses' anxiety transmitted itself at once to their riders, increasing their nervousness and sense of foreboding.

About halfway to the Mooncastle, the moonhorses faltered. Their wings began to dip and rise erratically, losing their rhythm. Their muscles strained against some gathering force, and their mouths began to foam. The children clung on, deeply alarmed, desperately trying to coax their steeds forward, yet feeling utterly helpless.

Then a great swirl of black fog swept down and enveloped them. The moonhorses were powerless to clear it. They reared and neighed wildly and seemed to the children to be in imminent danger of plunging to their deaths. But suddenly, with a powerful gust, the current of the fog pushed them round and sent them hurling off in the opposite direction; it was so strong, so purposeful, they had no need to flap their wings. Their riders clung on grimly. They glided swiftly through darkness like great, silent bats, in the grip of a force they could not comprehend.

The current swept them over the city. Above the Square, it suddenly ceased, and in the startling silence they drifted down. It had been too dark for the moonhorses or their riders to see where they were flying; and to find themselves suddenly in so familiar a place was a surprise and a relief. The dense, roaring currents swirled up and away, leaving behind the usual soft, grey, clinging fog, which seemed like balm in comparison.

They checked to see that everyone was all right. Their faces showed the strain of their ordeal, and the horses were sweating and shivering.

Why had they been brought here? They huddled together and tried to answer that. Should they try and take off again and fly to the Mooncastle? But they could see the moonhorses were not up to it. Perhaps the Diamond Horse was to meet them here? They could not agree on what to do and decided to form the usual circle and wait.

The moonhorses' shivering subsided into a tremble; they seemed to gain a little strength. Their moonstones still flickered, but perhaps the light was a little stronger. They flapped their wings in rhythm and slowly the fog cleared from the Square.

People gathered around the edge of the Square, and word soon spread through the city of the extraordinary sight to be seen there. Already awake and expectant, for this was – or should be – Fogclear Night, they gathered, murmuring excitedly. Some of the children tried to approach the moonhorses, but feeling the horses' distress, they had the sense to hold back.

Will climbed out of Jessie's pocket and settled in his hair. He knew that something momentous was about to happen, and he was determined to see everything so that he could report back to the twins.

A cold wind whipped up. People wrapped their cloaks and shawls and habits more tightly around themselves and shivered. Then with one accord, they looked up. The air was clearing. The wind was shredding the fog high up and wiping it out of the sky. A dark blue sky stretched over them; stars became visible.

But that was not what attracted their attention, or made them gasp and point, nor what caused their hearts to palpitate.

The fog had obscured most of the eclipse, and until now they had not been aware that it had happened. Yet now, as the fog cleared, the last of the eclipse was still visible, there was no mistaking it. They all feared eclipses of the moon, they knew what the legends said. They scanned the skies with increasing nervousness.

And then they caught their first sight of the Horse of the Eclipse with his Dark Rider. Nothing but a tiny, dense patch of darkness at first; but the truth dawned on them, and they grew silent. It made them think of a huge bat, or some mythical monster; and yet in the uncertain light from the stars and the moon they were kept wondering.

And they were puzzled by something else, too. What was that long white thing, dangling from its back leg?

The creature came nearer and nearer. Now they could clearly see a flying horse and a rider. But their attention was divided between it and that creature dangling from it. What was it? It looked like – of all things – an oversized infant! But how could that be?

Will alone recognized her. He laughed delightedly to himself, not because he liked the Child, but because he knew that with her around, Badrur – for he could see who the Dark Rider was – would not, after all, have things all his own way.

Suddenly, there was a cry of shock from the crowd. The Horse shook himself violently and the Child, taken by surprise, lost her grip. The crowd watched her plummet to the ground, shuddering as they imagined the impact in the trees.

Now all their attention was on the steed and its rider. "The Horse of the Eclipse," was on everyone's lips, making a strange, clipped, whispering, fearful sound pass through the crowd.

They grew still as Badrur and the Horse approached. Parents clutched their small children tightly. Stray cries were heard; metal spurs were clasped desperately. They could see every detail of the beast now: the dark underbelly, the flashing hooves, the flaring nostrils, the glossy feathers of its wings; but more important was the impression he gave of a concentration of darkness, of compacted fog and shadow. The Horse looked down and they saw the jet oval in his forehead, glinting like a malevolent third eye.

The moonhorses trembled. They hung their heads and felt their limbs grow weak. The Ancient Riders sat paralysed, caught between a fearful fascination for what was above them and an acute anxiety for their moonhorses.

The Horse of the Eclipse landed on the mosaic of the Spurs in the centre of the Square. He folded his glittering dark canopy of wings.

Some of the crowd were so overcome at the sight of him – images had existed of the Horse in their nightmares and deepest fears since early childhood, fed by endless lurid stories – they passed out or fled. Others huddled together in fear, finding comfort in a crowd.

The Ancient Riders realized at last the true extent of the danger they were in. They tried to urge their moonhorses to break away, but their steeds were too cowed in the presence of such a horse to respond. The children looked at one another in the knowledge that the pattern of the world as they knew it was broken.

The Horse struck a hoof on the mosaic. The sound was like the crack of a whip. The moonhorses shuffled forward, heads bowed, and formed a semi-circle in front of the great black beast. They lifted their heads. The Horse turned to the moonhorse at the end of the semi-circle on his left, and a beam of intense darkness shot from his jet stone. It hit the moonstone; the flickering light went out. The moonhorse sagged, as if the life-force had been drained out of it.

The Horse turned to the second moonhorse on his left. This was Astar's horse. She tried to lean forward to shield the moonstone, but the beam of darkness knocked her hand away and gave her such a shock only a desperate clinging to her moonhorse's mane stopped her from falling.

One by one the moonhorses were disabled.

When the last had been robbed of its light, all the moonhorses bowed down before the Horse of the Eclipse.

And then came the worst moment of all. As the moonhorses bowed, all the Ancient Riders felt suddenly that they no longer belonged. A message drummed through their heads: *Get off my back, you have no further right to ride me.* They looked at one another in bewilderment and dismay. They tried to resist the powerful feeling of rejection that passed through them, but it was no good. Soon they were involuntarily falling or climbing from their moonhorses.

Badrur laughed heartily, the sound of it bouncing off the Sanctuary building and echoing back at them. "They are nothing more than flying horses now," he mocked. "And you are no more than children. Go on, get out of here. You have no place here any more."

The children gathered in an anxious knot, powerless and afraid. They felt trapped between the weight of silence in the crowd and the concentration of darkness in the Horse.

An extraordinary hush fell on the scene. What was going to happen next?

There was a stirring of movement on the steps of the Sanctuary building behind the Horse. Most of the Councillors were on their estates, but the two of them who were in the city – Jessie's father, Councillor Torke, and Astar's mother, Helyna, now restored to vigorous health – appeared with a little retinue.

"What is going on here?" Helyna called out in ringing, imperious tones.

She was answered by silence.

The Horse of the Eclipse turned to face her.

Torke trembled, and Helyna went pale: they both recognized at once whom they were addressing.

The Horse neighed. It was like the trumpet of victory, full of arrogance and mockery. And then the most terrifying thing of all happened.

Dark ribbons of fog suddenly streamed from the beast's flared nostrils. They poured out one by one. Once in the air, the ribbons of fog twisted and turned and expanded, shaping themselves into an unmistakable sight: *moonghosts!* Hollow black eyes, pulsating mouths, writhing hands, a stench of cloying dankness: this was the first time they had been seen so clearly in the moonlight. Nothing was more frightening.

The people, until now spellbound, shuddered to their senses; shrieking their horror, they fled in all directions.

Some of the moonghosts drifted towards the knot of children. Terrified, they scattered. Only Jessie and Astar hesitated: even at this defining moment, they could not bear to part with their moonhorses. And as they clung to each other, trembling and defiant, moonghosts bore down on them with malevolent grins. But then, mysteriously, they veered away from them, a look of recoiling fear on their ghastly faces.

Astar guessed at once. "The pendants," she said. "They don't like them."

Jessie held his pendant out in front of him and bravely advanced towards a moonghost. The shadowy creature twisted away from him with a sudden spurt. "You're right," he said to Astar. "They can't get at us."

By now most of the crowd had fled, pursued by moonghosts.

From across the Square Astar and Jessie heard Badrur demand, "Open the doors to the Sanctuary." They saw their parents ineffectually try to bar the way, then stagger aside as moonghosts threatened them.

The Horse of the Eclipse mounted the steps and passed through the great double doors with Badrur still on his back.

The two children raced towards their parents, pathetically grateful that they were there. In the ante-chamber to the inner sanctum, where the left Golden Spur was kept, there was a brief reunion between them.

Inside the Sanctuary, the guards, pale and fearful, formed a wall in front of the Spur. They held out swords, daggers, spears.

"Out of our way," Badrur demanded contemptuously.

The guards brandished their weapons. "No one touches the Spur," the Captain of the Guard shouted.

The Horse of the Eclipse had an easy answer to that, one he plainly took delight in. He breathed out more moonghosts. The hideous grey apparitions fastened themselves on to the guards and smothered them. The guards screamed and writhed in horror, before they were silenced.

Astar and Jessie clung to their parents, hiding their faces from such a terrifying and sickening sight. Will looked on grimly; he was determined that whatever happened he would see it all for the twins' sake. How grateful he was that they had not been subjected to all this.

Badrur dismounted. He picked up a discarded sword and sliced through the golden chain that held the Spur in its stand. Catching the glass pendant as it fell, he held up the Spur. A thrill of such dimensions coursed through him, he had to gasp for breath and, once again, to steady himself against the stone plinth.

He tried to free the Spur from its glass casing. He slashed at it with his sword, but the blade bounced off. He hit it against the plinth, but that made no impression on it. He stared at it in growing frustration and surprise. The Horse neighed, then he lifted his left hoof. Badrur understood. He placed the Spur in its glass pendant on the ground in front of the Horse. The beast brought his hoof down and smashed the glass with one blow.

Badrur lifted the left Golden Spur and showed it triumphantly to all present. Then he fixed it to his left ankle. He admired it for a moment and chuckled to himself. One down, one to go. It was only a matter of time.

He remounted the Horse and the beast clattered back outside, down the steps and into the Square.

"I have one of the Golden Spurs," he shouted. "When I find the other, I shall be more powerful than anyone on the Four Islands."

It was something he had told himself countless times; it should have sounded triumphant. But in the silence of an almost deserted Square, it sounded a hollow boast, mockingly so. Angrily, he turned to the two Councillors on the steps of the violated Sanctuary. "Where is the right Golden Spur?" he shouted.

They could only reply with helpless shrugs.

He fixed his gaze on Jessie and Astar. Where were Tancred's brats, he wondered. Had they been here and fled with the others? He hadn't seen them. But if anyone could lead him to the right Golden Spur, it would be them. "Where are Tancred's twins?" he demanded of the two children.

"Gone," said Jessie.

"Hiding in the forest," Astar lied. "You'll never find them."

Badrur curled his lip. "I'll find them," he answered. "And then I'll soon squeeze the truth out of them."

He turned to Torke and Helyna. "Summon a meeting of the Ruling Council. I will address them as their master."

The Horse of the Eclipse was getting restless. Badrur patted him and said with a grim laugh, "My steed wishes to exercise a little of his power. He wants to breathe moonghosts throughout the city and in the Estates. Well, that's what he's here for, isn't it, and who am I to protest?"

With a bloodcurdling laugh, he spurred the beast. "I shall be back before long," he shouted. "Be ready." The beast flapped his great, black, glistening wings, creating waves of dark air, and they rose into the night, merging into the starlit darkness. As soon as they had gone, the fog seeped back into the Square.

Jessie and Astar pressed themselves against their parents in relief. They were both shaking.

"I'm so glad you're safe," said Helyna.

"This is what saved us," said Jessie. "The pendants I asked my mother to give to the twins; the twins lent them back to us. We always knew there was something special about them, but we never guessed they were to protect against the moonghosts. Or at least I didn't."

"They've been in our family for many generations," said Torke. "We were the first Estate – we think they've been with us since the beginning." His brow furrowed with anxiety. "We must try and think what to do."

"I want to get back to the twins," said Astar. "Before Badrur finds them. We have to give the pendants back. They may be their only protection."

"I can't let you go," said Helyna.

"We have to," said Jessie. "Father, you see that."

His father looked his son in the eye, then nodded briefly. "You should be safe on your moonhorses." He turned to look at the two that were still standing there. "Assuming they can still fly. But you must promise me that you will return at once as soon as you have warned the twins. We must find their father, too. He has gone missing."

"The school will soon be prey to those hideous moonghosts," Helyna warned. "Everyone will take their children away from it. It'll be a deadly place."

"Come on, Astar," said Jessie. "Let's see if our moonhorses can still fly."

The beasts were listless and fearful. Their wings were limp and lifeless. The children mounted them, but they hung their heads as if ashamed of their own weakness. In a moment of inspiration, Astar pressed the golden pendant next to her moonhorse's moonstone. The light flickered back on and regained its strength. The horse shivered once as if tossing off some dark skin, and flapped its wings. Astar sighed with relief; she knew she had regained her steed.

Jessie did the same.

They waved to their parents, promising a speedy return.

Will clung to Jessie's hair and thought, *This is only the start of it!*

CHAPTER 10

There were extraordinary scenes on the banks of the lake and around the school later that night. With so many moonghosts drifting through the city streets, many of the inhabitants fled into the surrounding woods and into the grounds of the Estates; but the parents of the schoolchildren made straight for the school.

At the lake's edge, there was a scramble for the few available boats; when they had set off across the water, the ferry boats were commandeered. The parents massed outside the tall, forbidding walls of the school. They hammered on the stout doors and shouted for their children.

Inside, there was near panic. "No child in this school," Mr Groak decreed, stomping up and down the corridors and stairs, "will leave here until the fog clears." The staff did not dare to question this. They locked the children in their dormitories on the third floor.

The children peered out of the barred windows at their parents, and grew frantic.

Cassie and Keiron had gone up on the roof very early to await the return of the Ancient Riders, and so they escaped this incarceration. They guessed that something terrible had happened in the city. They searched among the crowd below for any sign of their father, but with so much fog about, they could hardly make out individual faces.

And then, to their delight, Astar, Jessie and Will returned. They alighted on the roof as if out of nowhere, clearing the fog around them, bathing them in the soft milky light of the horses' moonstones. Everyone below paused to watch the moonhorses.

But the twins' joy evaporated when they heard the children's story. Badrur in the ascendant, the Horse of the Eclipse breathing moonghosts, the left Golden Spur seized: this catalogue of horrors was almost too much to take in.

"Luckily we had these," said Jessie, taking off his golden spur pendant with some reluctance and handing it back to Keiron. Astar, with a sigh, put hers around Cassie's neck.

And that's not all, said Will.

Not all? It's enough, said Keiron grimly.

Then I shan't mention it.

What?

You want to hear?

Yes!

The Child. She's back.

What? You've seen her?

Yes. She was hitching a ride with the Horse of the Eclipse, until she was shaken off over the forest.

Where?

Not far from here, I should think.

Should he tell Cassie? Keiron wondered.

"You must come back to our Estate," Astar was saying to Cassie. "It'll be safer there – if anywhere is safe on this island now."

"But my father? He might be here." Cassie peered over the edge of the roof again in desperate hope at the milling crowds below.

"We'll wait, then," said Astar. "But if he's not here, you will do as I suggest? You can't stay here."

Cassie nodded.

They worked their way around the perimeter of the roof – for the crowd had surrounded much of the building by now, looking for a way in – peering over the parapet in search of their father.

He was fretting on the other side of the water.

In the library of one of the Estates, Lord Tancred had come across a book of prophecies. It had cryptic numbers denoting auspicious dates in the future. From these he had worked out that the eclipse was imminent.

It gave him the impetus he needed to break away from the life of an itinerant storyteller that he had been obliged to live in the past weeks. It had not been hard to get permission to visit his children for Fogless Day; after all, as a parent, it was his right. He borrowed a horse, and was given an Estate worker to guide him; they set off through the foggy forest to the school. Whatever the law of the land, he was determined he would rescue his children and be with them at the perilous time of the eclipse.

On the night he had expected the fog to clear, he was on a knoll that rose above the trees. There he saw, with a shiver, the Horse of the Eclipse with his Dark Rider pass directly overhead, heading towards the city. He saw the Child, too, though from a distance he did not recognize at first who or what it was. He saw her being shaken free and heard her crash to the ground not far away.

These were disturbing sights, and when the fog swirled around him again, he hardly knew what to do. His guide had lost his nerve and was crouching useless at the foot of a tree, his head in his hands.

Some hours later, he heard something large and heavy crashing through the trees not far away. It was making too much noise for an animal. There was an odd sound too, half moaning, half humming – and suddenly he realized what it was. The Child! That huge and destructive infant that Cassie had helped bring into the world, that had followed them like a bad conscience from one island to another. For a minute he laughed grimly to himself – as if he hadn't got enough troubles!

But what if he could make use of her? All that brute strength – it might help him to get into the school and rescue his children. Was she a danger to him? Was it a risk he could take? He thought of the impenetrable doors and walls and windows of the school, he saw his twins, whom he sorely missed, with their faces pressed against bars, imploring him to come... Extraordinary measures were needed.

He stood on the knoll and called for the Child. She fell silent; then the crashing became louder as she headed in his direction.

The guide, terrified, was all for fleeing. Tancred had to twist his arm behind his back and threaten him with worse evils to make him stay.

The Child pushed aside the nearest trees and lumbered into view. She peered at the two men, puzzled, perhaps disappointed that it wasn't who she hoped it would be; then recognizing Tancred, she smiled and came forward. For a moment Tancred was afraid she might try and hug him, even stoop and give him a wet kiss, but instead she flopped down a few feet from him. There was a lot of mud on her ragged clothes and bits of bramble and leaves in her straggling hair. She had bruises on her legs and arms too, perhaps marking where she fell.

"Badrur," she murmured to herself. "Badrur." Then she pointed to the sky. "Horse." A look of sadness passed over her face.

So Badrur *is* the Dark Rider, Tancred thought in a flash. If that were so, he had no time to lose. The prince would be bound to make for the twins as soon as he learnt that they were in the school.

He walked warily towards the Child. Pointing in the direction of the school, he said "Badrur. That way. Badrur. Yes?"

Her face lit up.

"Come," said Tancred to the cowering guide. "Lead us to the school as quickly as you can."

Above the muffled din of the crowds below, the twins heard a loud splash. They couldn't see what had caused it, but they listened and heard the sound of rhythmic splashing growing louder, as if from the movements of a giant, clumsy swimmer. Keiron guessed who it was. It was time to tell his sister.

Her face went very white at first. She leaned against

the parapet and said in a strained voice, "Oh, not this. I can't bear it. Why has she come? Why doesn't she leave us alone?"

"I don't know," said Keiron, putting his arms around her trembling shoulders. "But we're safe from her up here, aren't we."

"We're not safe from her anywhere!"

"Who is she?" Jessie asked.

Keiron peered over the parapet. "Remember the Child we told you about? Well, look," he said, pointing below.

Through the fog, they could just see the Child clamber dripping on to the bank. Parents nearby looked at her with horror, screamed and scattered. She was used to that reaction now, and hardly noticed it; her one thought was to find Badrur. She pounded on the nearest door, shouting his name.

The children heard Mr Groak shouting back from a window below them, telling her angrily to go away.

The Child beat harder on the door. Everyone heard it crack and give way.

Mr Groak protested loudly; fear crept into his voice.

Word spread rapidly through the crammed dormitories that some kind of giant or monster was breaking into the building. On the roof, the four children could hear the screams of panic among their friends below.

"We'll have to go down and tell them what's happening," said Astar. "Are you coming, or do you want to stay here with the moonhorses?"

"Stay with them," Keiron urged his sister.

Cassie was not a faint-hearted girl, but she had suffered much at the hands of this Child; the creature had, after all, killed her best friend, Tara the wolf-girl. She nodded, then positioned herself between the two moonhorses, and clasped their silvery manes. She watched the other three disappear down into the school.

It appeared that most of the staff had bolted, by hidden passages known only to them, to escape the angry parents; but Mr Groak and Miss Rictus were wedded to the building and would not dream of deserting it even under the most extreme provocation. Their loyalty was to be tested to the limit.

The three children made first for the dormitories, hoping to find some way to free the rest of the children locked in there. They found Miss Rictus in the little antechamber where the door was, keeping guard.

"How dare you!" she shrieked. "Get back into the dormitory." She lunged at Astar with her long, bony fingers, her face livid, but the girl twisted away. She seemed like a madwoman: they did not feel like taking her on; besides, there was no sign of the key to the dormitory passage.

They escaped down the stairs to the classrooms, the woman's imprecations stinging their ears. Here they paused. Someone was coming up from the ground floor.

Mr Groak! Red-faced and out of breath, he glared at them furiously, bellowed at them to get back to their dormitory, then hurried as fast as his great bulk would allow him past the classrooms towards the Hall. In truth, with the Child in the building, he did not know where to run. He tried to barricade the door.

The children were half way down the next flight of stairs when they heard the Child. Frustrated at not immediately finding Badrur, she was getting impatient, and had started swiping at things in her path. The children heard the noise of furniture being tossed aside; they turned and fled back up the stairs. They took refuge in their classroom, crouching down to hide.

They heard the Child thump up the stairs, pause, then lumber down the passage. "Badrur," she was saying, "Badrur here." In the window of the door they saw her face, large, white, grizzling, but she passed on.

They heard the sound of a door crashing open and then silence.

"She's gone into the Hall," Jessie whispered. "Shall we bolt for it?"

"No," said Astar. "That's where Groak is. I want to see what she does to him." There was a note of such hate – and satisfaction – in that sentence, the two boys looked at her in surprise. "Well," she said in defence of herself, "he's deprived us of our freedom for years, and bullied us all. He deserves it, remember."

"Come on, then," said Keiron. "Let's see."

They stole along the passage towards the Hall. This was where the school gathered on formal occasions, where Mr Groak delighted in haranguing the children and stamping his brutal authority on them. They could hear him shouting as they approached. Peering round the door, they saw him behind the table on the dais, leaning forward bellowing threats, his great fists pounding the table, beads of sweat scattering from his whiskers as he shook his balding head. It was a bravura performance of bluster, fear and force.

The Child scowled. There was no Badrur here. Only this noisy and irritating man. She picked up a chair and hurled it at Mr Groak to shut him up. It hit him on the head and he staggered back, his face a picture of outrage. The Child laughed and threw another chair. Mr Groak fell; he hit his head on the edge of the table and passed out. That was lucky for him, for the minute he became unconscious, the Child lost interest in him.

She turned and saw the children. Astar and Jessie felt paralysed by her dark gaze. Never having seen her before, they were in awe at her size, the wildness of her black hair, the rags that draped her body, and, above all, the aura of destructive power that they sensed around her.

Keiron, having seen her several times before, was less intimidated. He stepped forward, wondering if she would recognize him.

She did. She pointed and smiled.

"Badrur," he said. "This way," and he gestured to her to follow him. A few blows of that fist, he reasoned, would soon knock the dormitory door down – that was his instantly formed plan; he did not have time to think beyond it.

The Child moved towards them. Astar and Jessie fled. Keiron shouted after them, "Go down and tell the parents what's happening."

He led the Child along the corridor and up the stairs towards the dormitory.

On the landing above stood Miss Rictus. She began to shout at Keiron as soon as he came into view; but then her words froze in her mouth when she saw the Child. Her face crumbled; she tottered, grasped the stair rail, steadied herself. "What is that?" she croaked in horror. Not waiting for an answer, she fled up the stairs to the roof.

Keiron smiled in relief: that was one obstacle out of the way. He pressed himself against one of the walls and pointed to the stout dormitory door. Inside, he could hear the children, some talking, some crying. He had the impression that some of them were pressed against the door, trying to hear what was going on. "Stand back," he shouted. "We're going to break the door down."

The Child filled the anteroom; she had to bow her head to get inside. "Badrur?" she said pointing at the door.

Keiron nodded. He was shaking all over now, and sweating. Never had he been so close to her. He knew that her touch could be deadly: all she had to do was wish her prey to be dead and it was. She reached out a finger towards him almost in affection, then at a noise from the other side of the door, she turned her attention to that. She pushed at the door. Finding it resisted her, she thumped on it hard. There was a splintering sound, but the door held.

Keiron slid round the wall until he was behind her. He watched the door crack and cave in under her powerful blows.

And then a cold shiver ran down his back. What would she do when she discovered Badrur wasn't there? She might be angry, like she was with Groak. Hadn't he put the children in danger?

What a fool he had been. What should he do?

He saw some parents creeping up the stairs. But they would be just as vulnerable.

Cassie! She was the only one who could get them out of this one. Her sister had given this Child life; there was something special between them. He raced up the stairs to the roof.

There a curious sight met him.

Cassie was standing between the two moonhorses, a hand on each mane. She was looking down contemptuously at Miss Rictus who had fallen to her knees in front of them. And Miss Rictus was blubbering! Great, obscene tears were running down the deep furrows of her dead white face. "I did not know," she was saying. "The moonhorses. Here." She kept her head low, unable to bear the light of the creatures. "I did not know that you and your brother were Ancient Riders. I thought you were just foreigners ..."

"Would it have made any difference, Miss Rictus?" Cassie interrupted, disgusted at this show of remorse. She could understand that the woman had been overcome by the sight of the Child and the moonhorses, and by the disruption of her little world, but she could not stomach the tears. "You envied the children in your class, didn't you? You couldn't bear to think they were better than you!"

"Let me just touch them," Miss Rictus pleaded, reaching out towards the moonhorses. They shied away.

"Go away, Miss Rictus," Cassie hissed. "You're not wanted here any more."

Miss Rictus's blubbering stopped instantly. She rose and staggered back. She pointed a sharp nail at Cassie and her face grew ugly. "It's your fault." She saw Keiron and swivelled her finger to point at him too. "Both of you. The minute you came here... Oh, I knew it from

160

the start. Spoilt, wicked *foreigners.*" This last she hissed with venom. Then something seemed to snap inside her. Consumed by a blinding hate, she lost control of herself. She cast about wildly for a weapon and found a loose slate.

"Look out, Cass!" Keiron called.

Miss Rictus flung the slate. Cassie ducked, and it just missed her. It hit the flank of one of the moonhorses. The creature neighed in pain. The other moonhorse reared on its hind legs, then snorting its anger, it advanced towards Miss Rictus. She staggered back in terror. "Get back," she cried. "Get back." But the moonhorse wanted revenge. It pushed the gesticulating woman towards the parapet; she was powerless to stop it. At the wall, the creature reared up again. Miss Rictus screamed, held up her hands to shield herself, leaned back too far, and tipped over.

The twins heard a splash. She was lucky to have fallen from a part of the building that jutted into the water. They saw her splashing frantically about in the dark water. Was she sinking or swimming? They had no time to watch, for there was a lot of screaming coming from the floor below.

"It's the Child," Keiron said. "I got her to break down the dormitory door."

"But she'll scare them all to death," Cassie said, horrified.

Keiron shrugged, shamefaced. It seemed a good idea at the time. "Cassie, could you..."

She knew what he meant. Her face, her fists, her soul clenched up, and she suppressed a piercing scream of rage and fear. Would her life always be dogged by this monstrous Child?

It was over in a minute. She knew she had no choice.

Before she left, she ran her hands over the spot where the slate had hit the moonhorse, and the creature felt the pain fade away. Then she patted the moonhorses in farewell. Pausing at the top of the stairs to gather her courage, she descended, her brother right behind her.

They had to fight their way through a congestion of frantic people in the antechamber. The door to the dormitory gaped wide, shattered by the Child's blows. There was so much pushing and crying and panic, it was hard for the twins to keep their heads.

The Child blundered into sight at the end of the dormitory corridor. She had not found Badrur. Her fists were clenched, her face was mulish; disappointment was turning to anger. Then, as the last of the crowd cleared between them, she saw Cassie. She went quiet and still. A deep memory stirred in the bottom of her heart, a memory of staring into that girl's eyes the minute she had come alive, of an attachment that made her want to both laugh and cry. She closed her eyes, as if trying to recall where and when she had seen the girl; but all that came into her mind was a mountain of monsters twitching in death and the jaws of a snapping wolf-girl. Then she remembered a cave of gushing water and a castle of mud.

Cassie was shaking all over. The Child always had this effect on her, but she steeled herself. She knew she only had to keep her distracted for a few minutes to allow the last of the children to escape.

"Get out. Quick as you can," Keiron was shouting to the children and their parents behind him.

"Badrur?" the Child said, her face growing sulky.

Cassie felt a flicker of pity for her. She shook her head, pointed at herself and said, "Cassie. I am Cassie."

The Child took a step forward. "Cassie," she repeated. "Cassie."

Keiron, not to be outdone, stood by his sister's side, and pointing at himself, said his name. The Child repeated it.

She chanted, "Cassie, Keiron, Cassie, Keiron," and thumped her feet in rhythm on the floor. Then she took another step forward, reaching out to them as if to clasp them. The children backed away. She didn't like that, and she scowled.

"Careful," Keiron whispered. "One false move..."

Hold hands, said Will urgently.

Why?

Because of the Spurs around your necks. They make a pair. Protection.

The Child lunged towards them. At the same time, Keiron grasped his sister's hand. They felt a crackling sort of power course through them. The Child was upon them, her pudgy fingers got within an arm's length of them before they slid away. The Child looked at her hand in surprise, then tried again.

The twins backed away, their hearts thumping hard.

Meawhile, their father, having at last got across the lake, had hurried against the tide of people to get into the school. Jessie noticed him in the crowd on the stairs. "Lord Tancred," he shouted above their heads. "The twins are with the Child. Follow me."

Tancred saw the splintered door in the antechamber, and climbed through it.

"Father!" Keiron exclaimed, amazed and delighted at his sudden appearance. Cassie thought her knees would give way when she saw him. They backed slowly towards him, keeping a wary eye on the puzzled Child. He gathered them into his arms.

The Child stretched out her hands and touched the corridor walls to steady herself. That feeling of belonging in some way to these three people puzzled her, set up a vague yearning in her heart.

"We'll send her up on to the roof," Tancred said, slowly backing towards the door with his children.

"The moonhorses are up there," Cassie whispered, catching her breath.

"Jessie and Astar will have flown away with them by now," said Keiron.

"Get behind me now," said Tancred. "Run downstairs as soon as you have the chance."

He pushed them behind him and stood before the towering child. "Badrur," he said, pointing upwards. "On the roof."

A while later, they were on a crowded ferry heading towards the bank. Looking back at the school, gaunt and shadowy in the swirling fog, they saw the Child lumbering about on the roof crying for Badrur. In their minds' eye, too, they saw Groak dead or unconscious at the foot of the Hall table; they saw the classrooms and dormitories smashed; they saw Miss Rictus slowly being pulled down into the inky lake by the weight of the water in her clothes.

"Where to now?" Keiron asked.

"To the city," said Tancred.

"But Astar said it's full of moonghosts, making everyone sick."

"So I've heard. There's only one thing – or one set of circumstances – that can stop the moonghosts taking over this island, with Badrur and the Horse of the Eclipse as its ruler."

"The Golden Spurs," said Keiron.

"And the Diamond Horse," said Cassie.

"That's about it," said Lord Tancred. "I'm afraid, my brave and long-suffering children, our adventures are not over yet."

Chapter 11

The twins and their father toiled through the damp and fogbound streets.

The moonghosts, drifting in and out of the fog, glared at them with hollow eyes but did not approach them for fear of the golden pendants.

"This gives a whole new meaning to the term 'ghost town', doesn't it," Keiron said with a grim smile.

The only sound in the muffled city was the coughing of those left behind, too sick to move from their beds.

It's like a blight on a whole forest, Will observed gloomily. He had come to hate this island so much, he spent much of his time sulking in Keiron's pocket. *Everything is turning mildewed.*

"The town is full of the dying," said Tancred. "The moonghosts are doing their work. At this rate, they'll be the only inhabitants left."

"Which is what Badrur wants, isn't it?" Cassie said bitterly.

"What the Horse of the Eclipse wants," said her father. "And whatever dark god made him. Badrur is only their pawn, although I don't suppose he would agree with me."

"Are we going to Councillor Torke's house?" Keiron asked.

"We could stay there," said Tancred. "It's as good a place as any. We can work out what's the best thing to do once we're there."

They turned a corner and to their surprise they nearly bumped into a moonhorse. For a few seconds they did not recognize it as such, for it was laden down with baskets containing pungent dried herbs, bottles of liquid, packets of powders. It was tethered to the rail on a flight of steps of a house where subdued lights glimmered. Cassie stroked its muzzle. "I wonder who you belong to," she murmured, distressed to see a moonhorse being used like a packhorse.

Keiron knocked on the door. They heard someone hurry down the stairs. The door opened.

"Herbie!" Keiron exclaimed. "What are you doing here?"

"Keiron! Cassie! We wondered what had happened to you." Herbie, small, pale and tired-looking in the sickly light, grinned with relief to see them. "I'm doing what I can for the sick. It's my duty. I'm from the Estate of Medicine, remember? All my family are out in the city somewhere doing this."

"Are you having any success against the Cough?" Tancred asked.

Herbie shook his head despondently. "We can relieve the symptoms a bit, ease the pain, that is all."

"You must be careful, they'll try and get you too."

"They keep trying," Herbie said, grinning again. "But they're not too fond of the smell of the herbs about me." He drew close to them and whispered, "All the others are hiding, with their moonhorses. They have been waiting for you to return."

"Us? Why?"

"Because your pendants protected Astar and Jessie's moonhorses. That's what they told us. You can bring the rest of the moonhorses back to life. Besides, you're one of the Ancient Riders."

"Are they far?" Tancred asked.

Herbie shook his head.

"Then I think we'd better go to them now," said Tancred.

Cassie laid her hand on her father's arm. "I'm staying here, Father," she said. "I can't let all these people suffer when I can help them. Listen to them coughing. They're in agony."

"Are you sure?" her father asked tenderly. He was reluctant to let her out of his sight after being parted from her for so long.

"I have to," she said simply.

"Then you must work with Herbie." He turned to the boy, who nodded.

To guide them through the city, Herbie provided them with a sequence of different groove patterns to correspond with the grooves incised in the walls of each street.

Tancred gave Cassie a little hug.

"Look after yourself," said Keiron, sorry to be parting from her. "See you soon."

Cassie watched them disappear into the fog. She had an impulse to run after them, but she held herself back.

The moonhorse whinnied softly. "Of course," she murmured. "You want this, don't you?" and she held up her pendant. There were several hisses in the air around her, from unseen moonghosts, and Herbie drew nearer to her for protection. She placed the pendant next to the moonstone on the horse's brow: the light's feeble flickering turned into a strong milky glow. The children could feel the life-blood coursing back into the beast. It spread its wings, scattering baskets and bottles into the road. They danced about to avoid them, laughing.

"Fantastic," said Herbie, hugging his moonhorse. "You've given her back her life."

Cassie took a deep breath and composed herself. "Come on," she said. "Lead me to your patients. We've got a lot to do."

Keiron and his father groped their way down street after deserted street, their ears filled with the coughing of the sick, their clothes and hair dripping with the damp fog. They reached the outskirts of the city and became lost. Keiron resorted to the use of his gift, asking stones and walls who had come by here lately, until one said, *The Ancient Riders? Straight ahead.*

They came to tall double doors in a wall, similar to ones described by Herbie. "This must be it," Tancred muttered. They thumped on the doors and called out, but there was no answer.

"Let me climb on your shoulders," said Keiron.

He peered into a large stableyard. On the far side were shuttered stables. He thought he saw a light flicker in one of them for a second.

"I'll climb over," he said.

He fell on to cobbles and rolled over.

"I'll just take a look," he whispered to his father. He ran silently across to the stables and tried to look through a grimy window. He rubbed it, and the sound was magnified in the silence.

Then suddenly hands seized him, covered his eyes and mouth, dragged him into the building. A light was held up to his face.

"Keiron!" several voices gasped.

He had found them.

Silently, they unbolted the gate and let Tancred in.

The moonhorses were brought into the courtyard. Keiron held the golden spur pendant to their moonstones; the horses came back to life. They neighed softly, flapped their wings, and the fog in the stable-yard cleared.

How tired and bedraggled the Ancient Riders looked now! But they were happy, and several hugged Keiron in relief and gratitude. Will jumped out of Keiron's pocket, and they made a great fuss of him, as if he was a long-lost mascot.

"Where's Cassie?" Astar wanted to know.

Keiron explained.

The moonhorses were getting restless. "I think you should all return to your Estates," said Tancred. "Your families will be missing you, and you will be safer with them."

Several of the children made for their moonhorses at once, for this was their intention. But Jessie and Astar lingered.

"What's going to happen?" Jessie asked anxiously.

"I don't know," said Tancred. "Keiron and I are going to the Square to see if we can find out anything."

"That's where Badrur and the Horse of the Eclipse are," Jessie said. "In the Sanctuary."

"Is that so?" Tancred said softly.

"I think my father's still there, too. And Astar's mother. They're trying to reason with him, or something."

"Then we'll go to them at once."

Keiron turned to Astar. "What will you do?" he asked.

"I'm going to find Cassie. I may be able to help her."

"If we see your mother, we'll tell her," said Tancred. "In any case, meet us in the Square at nightfall. Tell Cassie. We'll all decide what to do then."

One by one the moonhorses took off and were swallowed up by the swirling fog. None of them knew when they would meet again, or under what circumstances, but they all sensed that this was only a temporary escape and that greater danger loomed ahead.

The light from Jessie's moonstone lit the way through the ghost-haunted streets towards the Square.

Keiron felt a persistent gnawing in his stomach, and eventually he couldn't help saying, "If I don't eat something soon, I'll faint!"

"Me too," said Jessie. "Let's go to my house first."

"Have we got time?" Tancred wondered, looking at the boys doubtfully.

"I want to go there, anyway," said Jessie. "It'll be the safest place for my moonhorse."

That decided it, and they were soon letting themselves into the yard at the back of the house. They left the moonhorse in a stable there. "We'll be back soon," said Jessie, stroking her nuzzle. "Keep quiet and still and you should be all right. We won't be long."

To their surprise, the old servant was still there, she had not fled with the rest of the population. In fact, she looked younger and healthier than she had been for a long time, and they stared at her in surprise. "I heard about your sister," she explained, looking at Keiron, "and although I was at death's door with my cough, I managed to drag myself to the house where she was laying on the hands. It's a miracle, no mistake. As soon as she touched me, the pain bled away; I took great gulps of air and felt as if I could float! Oh, it was wonderful. She said you'd be back soon. Come, you all look famished. Let me get you something to eat."

They settled thankfully around the dining-table and seized upon the food the minute she placed it in front of them.

"My sister's all right, then?" Keiron asked between mouthfuls.

"She never stops. Like one possessed. She flies from one house to another, as if time itself was at her heels."

"That sounds like Cass," he grinned.

"Did you see Astar arrive?" Jessie asked.

"That girl with the moonhorse and the wild hair?" Jessie nodded.

"Yes, not long before you came. Cassie was mighty pleased to see her, I can tell you. And the moonhorse: people got off their deathbeds to look at it as it went past their windows." She began to shuffle out, somewhat embarrassed by her own garrulous enthusiasm, but Tancred called her back and said, "Have you heard where the Dark Rider is?"

She scowled and shuddered. "In the Sanctuary," she said. "That's where he's set himself up." She clenched her fists. "And to think I led him from this very house to the Square, and queued with him to see the Spur. If I'd have known who he was. . ." Her face darkened, and she hurried out, leaving the three of them to wonder how that sentence might have been completed.

"Father," said Keiron. "Badrur and his Horse are the greatest power in the island now. What chance have we got against him?"

"None, by ourselves. But I do not believe the goddess Citatha has abandoned us."

"There is a power on this island greater than Badrur or his Horse," Jessie reminded them, his eyes flashing.

"The Diamond Horse?" said Tancred.

Jessie nodded vigorously. "He must know what is going on; he sees everything through his diamond."

"Then why doesn't he do something?" Keiron asked, baffled. "Why hasn't he appeared?"

"Because he's been waiting for you and Cassie," Jessie explained. "Together, you are his Rider. Once you come together, well, he'll be more than a match for Badrur and the Horse. You know this – and I'm sure your father does too." He looked searchingly at Tancred.

"I believe it to be so," said Keiron's father. "There are many books in the Estates' libraries which suggest as much. At any rate, you and Cassie must go to the Diamond Horse. You must finally take up your position as the twelfth and last Ancient Rider." He looked solemnly into his son's eyes. "I believe that everything will depend on you and your sister, Keiron. How, I am not sure. But the goddess Citatha will be there to protect you, be sure of that."

"Can we be sure of that?" Keiron muttered.

"Have faith, Keiron," Tancred said; then, seeing the doubt in his son's eyes, he added, "Who do you think made those spur pendants, if it wasn't her?"

Keiron looked down at his pendant, and he felt reassured.

"I believe my moonhorse, and Astar's, will take them to the Mooncastle," Jessie said. "All things have changed now; they know what is at stake, they won't refuse any more, especially if we, as their riders, insist on it."

Tancred pushed his plate away and stood up. "Then, as soon as we have found out how things stand in the Square, you and Cassie will fly to the Mooncastle. You must bring back the Diamond Horse. I believe that is our only hope."

"And the Golden Spur?" said Jessie.

"Ah, yes, the missing Spur," Tancred said, surprised that it had slipped his mind.

"Is it in the Mooncastle?" Keiron asked.

"No one knows," Jessie sighed. "But where else would it be? It's the one place on the island no one has ever been able to search."

"If it's there, you *must* find it," said Tancred, placing an urgent hand on Keiron's shoulder. "It may be the one thing that will make all the difference."

Keiron nodded solemnly. "And it is after all what we came here for," he added with a wry smile.

* * *

At the last minute, Jessie decided to stay with his moonhorse: with moonghosts swirling all around her, she was nervous and he felt she needed him.

They felt their way through the fog to the Square. It appeared to be deserted, but there were lights in the Sanctuary Building. They made their way to the back entrance. The guards had scattered long ago or had succumbed to the Cough. Badrur relied on the moonghosts to guard him.

"If I remember rightly, there's a balcony around the inner sanctum, where the Spur used to be," whispered Tancred. "We'll make for that."

They flitted unseen up a curved staircase and looked down into the circular chamber. Where the right Golden Spur had once stood was now a large, ornate chair which Tancred recognized as belonging to the Council Chamber. In it sat Prince Badrur. Beside him was the Horse of the Eclipse, his wings folded. In front of him stood Councillors Torke and Helyna.

Will and Keiron both shivered at the sight of the Horse. Its dark, glittering eyes seemed to be everywhere.

"I have listened to your pleas for long enough," Badrur was saying to the two Councillors. "And you speak most eloquently of your people's suffering. But you know there is only one thing that can overpower the Horse of the Eclipse and his moonghosts."

The Horse exchanged a flashing glance with his rider, in which there was a warning wrapped up in contempt. But Badrur returned the look with a sly one of his own.

Incongruously, he raised his left foot to display the Golden Spur. "The right Spur. That's all I want. That's all I – we – need to be master here. Find that for me – or point me to where it is hidden – and we have the basis for a bargain. Until then, all your words mean nothing to me."

The Councillors glanced anxiously at each other. "We believe that the other Spur is hidden with the Diamond Horse in the Mooncastle," said Helyna patiently. "But we cannot send our children there because you have disabled their moonhorses."

Badrur shrugged. "Then I will go there myself."

"You won't find it," Torke said, shaking his head. "Only the moonhorses know how to get there. And you've disabled them."

Badrur rose from his chair and glared at them angrily. "The Horse of the Eclipse will seek out the Diamond Horse and destroy him," he shouted. "It is only a matter of time."

He dismissed them with a wave of his hand.

Night fell. As arranged, Tancred, the twins, Astar and Jessie met with their moonhorses in the Square, beneath one of the giant statues.

Cassie looked tired but extraordinarily happy.

"She's saved countless lives," said Astar, looking at her friend with awe.

"I'm exhausted!" Cassie added, stretching her arms and yawning.

"The moonhorse will soon revive you," said Astar. "Go on, jump up. You'll see."

"Are you sure? Will she let me?"

Astar was right. The light from the moonstone swirled up and an aura formed around her; she felt the strength of the light pass into her. "It's incredible," she laughed.

Jessie turned to Keiron. "Jump on to my horse." Keiron did so, and the light surrounded and passed into him too. "Oh, it's amazing! I feel as light as a feather, and as strong as a giant!" He laughed. "At last, I'm riding a moonhorse!"

"It's always like that for us," said Jessie, grinning. "On Fogclear Night."

It's like the first real day of Spring, said Will. *A dozen of them all rolled into one!*

"Father," said Keiron, his eyes glowing. "I think we should fly to the Mooncastle tonight. We should go now."

"Yes!" Cassie exclaimed, fired with the same sudden inspiration. "It's time we met the Diamond Horse."

Tancred nodded slowly. Yes, the time had come. He stood between the two horses and took his children's hands. "Do your best to find the missing Golden Spur," he said. "And come back with the Diamond Horse. The fate of the whole island is in your hands."

He let go and stepped back. "Farewell, my children. I hope when we meet again, we shall be triumphant."

Without another word, the twins urged their mounts to fly. The beasts flapped their great white wings, and rose, clearing the fog around them.

They were alone in the cold, fogbound heavens. The wind tore at them, the fog formed ghastly shapes around them, and time seemed to have no dimension here; but the strength from the light of the moonstones sustained them through this darkest of journeys.

CHAPTER 12

The twins flew through the grey, foggy expanses above the dark trees, aware that only the light and energy from their steeds kept them from being suffocated and frozen. The beasts' wings seemed no match for the kind of fog that now imperceptibly thickened above the island, but they beat strongly, and the light from their moonstones beamed into the menacing fog with defiant persistence.

Some time later Will said, *I can feel it.* He was clinging on to Keiron's hair, terrified of being snatched away by a gust of wind, but not wanting to miss anything of the journey.

What?

The Mooncastle! Ahead.

I can't see it.

Not yet.

A few minutes later they became aware of a pool of soft, cold, blue light penetrating the wall of fog ahead of them. It was so diffused that at first it looked merely like a lighter patch of fog; but it steadily gained in strength until it resembled a giant moon towards which they were flying. It was exhilarating. They felt the moonhorses put on a spurt; they saw the fog dissolve in the light.

The Mooncastle came into view, its towers first, glittering as if studded with blue stars, then its battlements and walls, radiating blue light. As they flew closer, fantastic details came into focus – carvings, ornate arches, moulded corbels, engraved shields, statues in niches – that all seemed sculpted from semi-translucent ice. As the twins descended towards the mysterious edifice, they saw that within its walls and all the elaborate details, a sort of blue-white mist swirled gently, like smoke in a bottle. It gave what should have been something monumental a feeling of insubstantiality. They soon discovered why.

The moonhorses alighted on a white stone path that led to a bridge. They would be safe: there were no moonghosts here.

The twins left them there and crossed the bridge. Below it flowed a crystal clear stream, its tinkling accentuated in the silence. The bridge led under a huge arch. The doors were open, and they stepped into a brilliant courtyard. Arches defined by fluted columns were ranged around three sides, and above that were balconies from which hung spears like icicles. The effect was dazzling.

It was extraordinarily quiet. Preternaturally so.

Cassie stepped into the centre of the courtyard, expectantly. Surely the Diamond Horse would appear to them now?

Keiron was fascinated by the swirling blue-white mist in the substance of the castle walls. He reached out to touch a wall and was amazed to find his hand passing through it. He cried out in surprise. He tried again. The same thing happened. The walls looked solid enough, but they appeared to be made of a sort of sculpted mist.

Moon mist, Will offered.

What's that?

That circle of misty light you sometimes get round the moon. It's that, I'm sure.

"Here, Cassie, come and put your hand through this," Keiron called.

Cassie shrieked her delight and terror when her hands passed through what looked like thick, glassy walls and doors and columns, and for a while they had quite a game of it, passing their whole bodies through solid-seeming planes. The cold and towering edifice echoed with their laughter.

But the Diamond Horse did not appear, and this soon sobered them.

Standing in the centre of the courtyard again, a sort of loneliness descended on them. It felt as if they had been transported to the moon, far away from anything they were familiar with, and the silvery silence pressed around them.

"Let's go inside," said Cassie.

They found a door under one of the arches and passed through it. Here there were empty corridors and rooms containing nothing but a bluish light. They came to some stairs. "Do you think we can walk on them?" Cassie asked. "Or will our feet pass through them?"

The stairs were made of what looked like transparent glass. They held the twins' weight, but with each step the children took, it became more and more nerve-racking: they did not dare to look down. They reached the first floor with a little panicky rush.

Here there was a giant hall, empty except for a long table in the centre. Carved in relief on the walls were huge life-size sculptures of the eleven moonhorses. Each had its Rider, and the twins wandered around the hall, identifying them, for the likeness of each was remarkable. How was this possible, they wondered, unless the carvings were recent, which seemed un-likely, or the substance of the walls changed to depict the advent of a new Rider.

They came to the biggest relief of all. It showed what was unmistakably the Diamond Horse, a great light radiating from the jewel in his head. On his back was the likeness of the twins. That shouldn't have surprised them, but it did. They shivered and instinctively clasped hands. It was eerie and magnificent. They felt uplifted by it, and yet, in mere flesh, insignificant in comparison to it, for it loomed majestically above them and seemed to speak of something far greater than anything they could imagine.

"It gives me the same feeling as the Golden Armour gives me," Keiron whispered.

"Me too."

"It's really true, then," he said in awe. "We *are* its Rider. I never fully believed it before."

"Nor me. It was always just something we were told. But now..."

They lingered for some time in this hall of carvings, hoping perhaps that it might reveal more of what they should do.

"We should keep looking," said Keiron at last. "There are still many more rooms above us."

"But I'm beginning to get the feeling that the Diamond Horse isn't here," Cassie said, giving her brother a look of despair.

"Perhaps he's gone. Couldn't wait any longer."

"But where?"

"To the city. He must have seen through his diamond what was going on."

"But why leave now? Why so late?"

Keiron shrugged.

"Anyway, we can't leave without the right Golden Spur," said Cassie, looking about her dubiously. "It's somewhere in this castle. It must be."

The building – if it could be called that – seemed suddenly huge and limitless, towering above them, room after room, passage after passage, like a series of endless echo chambers all around them.

Use your gift, Will suggested.

Table, said Keiron. *Where shall I find the Spur?*

The table replied, but because of the shifting quality of its substance, the answer that came back was scrambled and muffled, filling Keiron's head with a cacophony that grated on his nerves. It was the same with anything else he asked. What came back was like another language, he could make nothing of it.

"I'm sorry," he said to Cassie.

"We'll just have to go from room to room until we find it," said Cassie. "At least we know *roughly* where it is now. I mean, it's not lost in a vast forest, is it? That's an improvement!"

They trailed from room to room, hallway to stair,

through grand chambers, down endless passages. It was like being in a dream, the light buoying them up, the emptiness cleansing them; and yet at the heart of it they sensed a vacancy, a sadness, which pricked them on.

On the top floor there was a glassy hall. In the middle of it was a spiral staircase leading up into the highest tower. It appeared to have water running down it, although that was an illusion; climbing up it was like ascending a fountain.

"You know what this reminds me of?" Keiron said, a memory of another island, another search for a piece of the missing Golden Armour, flashing through his mind. "The fountain on East Island where we found the Shield. Remember?"

"Yes! And when we climbed to the top of it to free Will – how did he get stuck up there? I've forgotten – the whole thing collapsed. I hope this staircase isn't going to do the same."

Will's memory of that time was more painful. A bird had been stabbing him with a sharp beak, thinking he was a twig. The indignity of it had almost been as bad as the pain.

They reached the top of the staircase without mishap and emerged at the edge of a circular chamber. After the emptiness of the castle's rooms and halls, they were surprised to find something in the centre of this one. There was a table. On it lay a skeleton. Its bones were of the same glittering, misty substance as everything else. It seemed more peaceful than frightening, like an emblem of eternal sleep. The twins stared at it for some time, wondering if it might come alive. But it remained utterly still.

They noticed that the floor was like glass, clear and invisible.

Around the table there was a double circle etched in the glass. Inside the lines a message had been scratched, but the twins could not read it from where they stood.

They looked at the transparent floor. It appeared as if there was no floor at all in front of them, just a sheer drop to the shadowy hall below. Although the surface of their mind told them it was safe, all their instincts said, tread on that and you will plunge to your death.

Cassie put out a tentative foot, touched the transparent floor, and withdrew it quickly, nerves stabbing at her. Keiron tried too, and drew back just as quickly.

It's a test, Will observed.

Well, I've failed, Keiron said, looking anywhere but at the invisible floor.

Cassie had a second go. "I can't do it."

They froze, wondering what to do.

Keiron's gaze settled on the skeleton. Who was he? Or she? Why had their bones been preserved here?

"Cassie," he said suddenly, excitement quickening his voice. "What do you see on its heels? Am I imagining it, or is it. . .?"

"Yes!" Cassie cried, hardly daring to believe what she saw.

On the skeleton's heels was fixed a pair of golden spurs.

"Have we really found them?"

They pressed their hands together gleefully and cried, "Yes!"

But the twins' sense of triumph was soon checked by a sudden and inconvenient thought. Why *two* spurs? Surely there should only be one?

That's the test, said Will. *Or half of it.*

What do you mean?

I think you have to go over this floor and choose the right spur.

Well, the second part of that is easy. It must be the spur on his right foot.

Aren't you meant to think that? It's too easy.

"What's Will saying?" Cassie asked. He told her. "Then send him over to read that inscription. It might tell us for sure what we've got to do."

Will sauntered over the glassy floor, whistling. He had no fear of heights, and he knew that if he tumbled his wooden body would be no more than scratched in the fall. He reached the message, found where it began, then read it out to Keiron as he walked right round the circle in the floor.

"I am the first Ancient Rider. You are the last. We cross hands over the centuries. You must complete what I began. Cross the gulf of faith. Ask of each spur your deepest question. Choose the answer you think is the truth. If you are right, you will possess the missing Golden Spur. If you are wrong, all but the moonghosts and their master will perish on this island."

Will had to read it again slowly, twice, so they could be sure they had fully grasped its message.

"First," said Keiron, swallowing hard, "we have to cross this glassy floor."

"We have to cross the gulf of faith."

"It'll certainly need faith to cross that."

Close your eyes, Will suggested.

"Will says we should close our eyes."

"Yes, but is that having faith?"

Keiron shook his head. "Look ahead, then. Fix your eyes on the spurs."

"Don't look down. That's the answer," said Cassie. She clasped her hands together to stop them trembling. She was the first to put a foot out.

It was like walking on a sheet of glass over a ravine. At any moment, it might crack or shatter, and send them tumbling to their deaths. Never had they felt so scared.

"Take my hand," Cassie wailed.

If we're going down, we'll go down together, Keiron thought grimly. His heart was beating so hard, his whole frame seemed to shake.

Have more faith, Will said unhelpfully.

They shuffled forward. The expanse of invisible floor between them and the skeleton seemed to expand as they voyaged out. Fixing their eyes on the spurs helped, but as they neared halfway, their gaze began to wander. It fixed itself on the skull. That reminded Keiron of the skulls in the crypt beneath the Chapel on North Island, where he had once been trapped; it reminded Cassie of the empty visor in the Helmet through which she had seen all the petrified monsters around the Ice Castle at home stir into hideous life... These memories made them falter.

Come on, Will urged, knowing how dangerous such hesitations were.

But they slowed to a paralysing halt. Seemingly suspended in mid-air above a great drop, they felt as vulnerable as they had ever been in their lives. They were told to have faith: but faith in what? A skeleton? A thing of death?

"Help me," Cassie whispered, closing her eyes.

Help us, Will, Keiron pleaded desperately.

Will stared at them helplessly as they stood, frozen in mid-air. What could he do?

Something caught his eye in the shifting surface of the ceiling. Looking up, he saw the smoke-like shape of a cat, its eyes blue, its tail swishing. He remembered. In the past, when the twins were in severe danger, a Silver Cat had mysteriously appeared. It had been a long time since he had thought of her.

Think of the Silver Cat, he urged Keiron. *Picture it in your mind.*

Keiron did so at once, and the picture of the Silver Cat staring into his eyes immediately calmed him. Somehow, the picture transmitted itself to Cassie. She saw it, took a deep breath, smiled, and opened her eyes.

"Did you see the Cat?" she whispered.

Keiron nodded. "We can have faith in her."

They kept the image of the Silver Cat in their minds for the rest of that short but seemingly endless journey over the glassy floor to the skeleton. The twins leaned against the table and waited until their heartbeats slowed to normal.

"I expect we were perfectly safe on that floor," Cassie observed. "So why were we so scared?"

"Instinct," said Keiron. "We had to go against instinct to cross that gulf."

"I think I'd prefer a whole week of Miss Rictus's ghastly lessons to doing that again."

"Well, what now?"

They turned to the two golden spurs. "We have to choose the right one. By asking them our deepest question."

They stared at the spurs. They were identical: the ornate, engraved patterns on them, the shape of the wheel and the clasp, their beauty.

Then they looked searchingly at each other. What was their deepest question?

"I know what mine is," Keiron said after a pause, his face grave.

"Me too."

Always, there had been one central mystery about their lives. Their mother. Who was she? What had separated them from her in infancy? Was she alive or dead? Their father had remained mysterious about her, vague and troubled in all his answers to their enquiries. Well, that was their deepest question.

Gingerly, they unclasped the spurs from the skeleton's glassy ankles, and took one each.

"You ask first," said Cassie. She was trembling again.

Keiron looked at the spur glittering in his hands. With a lump in his throat, he said, "Who is our mother?"

A deep, hollow voice filled the room. It made them start and stare around, fearful. *"She was a beautiful princess,"* said the voice. *"From a far land. She was shipwrecked on Temple Island and rescued by your father. They fell in love. But she died giving birth to you, and now her likeness is worshipped in a hidden shrine. Your father grieves endlessly, unable to speak of her."*

They considered this in silence for a moment. "That could be true," said Keiron. "Don't you think?"

Cassie nodded. "It explains why Father never gives us a straight answer about her."

There was another silence. "I don't like to think of her as dead," Keiron said with a sigh. "I never have, though I suppose I should."

"Me, neither."

"Ask your spur."

Cassie clasped her spur tightly and closed her eyes. "Is she dead?"

The voice filled the room with the second of its two answers, from which they had to choose.

"Your mother was a priestess in Citatha's Temple. It was forbidden for her to take a lover, or marry: she had pledged all her love to the goddess. But she fell in love with your father; it was so powerful she was helpless to resist it. At your birth, Citatha punished her. She transformed her into a beast. A magical one, but a beast all the same. Your mother stalks the netherland between now and the hereafter, looking for a way back."

The twins looked deeply into each other's eyes, perhaps more searchingly than they had ever done in their lives, to see if either doubted which answer they should choose. The first answer seemed more realistic; it explained everything in the simplest of terms. But the second answer held out the prospect that she was alive, that they might conceivably be reunited with her. She might be suffering in that borderland between life and death, they knew that; but there was hope.

Keiron held out his spur and looked enquiringly at his sister. She nodded. He upturned his palm and let the spur drop. It passed silently through the glass and plummeted down through floor after floor. It travelled on down into the earth, into the furnace there, where it shrivelled up like a leaf on a fire.

"This is the true one," said Cassie, holding up the missing Golden Spur. It shone, fiery and gold, and they both thrilled at their sudden success.

The walk across the transparent floor held no terrors for them now, even though the fate of the false spur had shown them what might have happened to them if they had chosen the wrong one.

The Golden Spur, which Keiron hung around his neck, gave their moonhorses boundless energy. It banished the fog around them, clearing a great golden space through which they sailed; they skimmed over the dark forest on the wings of happiness. In their relief at finding the Spur, with their hearts filled with a new hope about their mother, they did not think too much of what might be awaiting them back in the fogbound city. They had not felt so much joy in a long time, and they were eager to bring the news to their father.

But as the roofs of the city loomed out of the fog, their joy slowly evaporated. The moonhorses hovered over the Square for a minute, where the fog had cleared, unsure where to land. Its perimeter was crowded. In the centre were two horses, facing each other a short distance apart, one black, one white.

The crowd turned to look at the twins as they landed not far from the two beasts. Astar and Jessie ran to them, thankful to have their moonhorses back safe and sound.

"Look," Astar pointed, awed and troubled. "It's been like this since soon after you left."

"It's a duel unto death," said Jessie, grimly.

The Horse of the Eclipse, his black coat glistening, his wings slowly flapping, was casting an intense beam of darkness at the other steed. Badrur sat astride his back, grim, determined, his eyes glaring. Around them, just catching the light, moonghosts hovered, keeping the citizens at bay.

Opposite stood the Diamond Horse, white, powerful, magnificent, his dark blue eyes steady, his great wings flapping. From the diamond on his forehead there beamed a shaft of sparkling light which, on meeting the beam of darkness half-way between them, created a fierce little ball of hissing sparks.

Both horses seemed invincible. They had been locked in this trial of strength for many hours. But breaking point was near. The Horse of the Eclipse had the power of the right Spur which constantly renewed his energy. The Diamond Horse had only his own finite strength – more powerful than darkness, as light always is, but running out fast. And without his rider, he was fatally weakened.

Lord Tancred worked his way through the rapt crowd to his children. "Did you...?" he said, barely daring to hope, for so much depended on their success. Keiron held up the Golden Spur. Tancred's face lit up. "Is it...? Can it be...?"

The twins laughed at the expression of delight and disbelief on his face. He took the Spur, pressed it to his lips, smiled ecstatically, then gave his children such a hug their breath was knocked out of them.

A gasp from the crowd made them turn. They saw the Diamond Horse suddenly falter. His right leg bent a little, and his beam of light began to flicker erratically. They watched in horror. Shadows began to appear on the horse's white fur, like the smudges on the moon.

Badrur laughed, a cruel, ecstatic laugh, and he threw up his arms in triumph.

"Go," Tancred urged his children. "You are the Diamond Horse's true rider. Fix the Spur to your ankle, Keiron. Quickly!"

The Spur clipped on easily. The twins raced across the Square. "We have the right Golden Spur," they shouted.

Badrur glowered at them. "Keep them away," he shouted, but no moonghost would dare approach them.

Close up, the Diamond Horse was huge, much bigger than a moonhorse, too big for them to mount unaided. The twins hesitated, suddenly overcome with awe and timidity.

"Climb on to his wings," Astar shouted across to them.

The Diamond Horse, unable to move his head to look at them, for fear of giving the Horse of the Eclipse the advantage he was looking for, lowered his wings. The twins clambered on to them and settled on his back. Cassie was behind, clasping her brother's waist. At once they felt suffused with light: it swept through them, erasing doubt and fear and tiredness and tension. They were at one with the beast.

The Diamond Horse, for his part, felt a surge of rejuvenating strength. His light beam steadied, the shadows on his fur faded; he neighed triumphantly across the Square, telling everyone that at last he had found the two-headed rider, halved but one.

Badrur felt the Horse of the Eclipse stiffen and hesitate. He shouted furiously at the twins. A few more minutes and he would have defeated the Diamond Horse, removing the last obstacle to complete power. But now... How he cursed them!

The two sides were even. Both with a Spur. They faced one another, the ball of sparks at the point where the light and dark met hissing like a fierce animal. The minutes ticked by with no change.

Deadlock.

Tancred suddenly despaired. This could go on for ever. What power on earth could break this? Light and dark, good and evil, life and death, locked together in a fierce embrace. He suddenly saw that he had placed his children in a hideous trap.

CHAPTER 13

The Child looked up. She saw what appeared to be a pool of golden light sailing through the fog. As it passed directly overhead, she saw inside it two moonhorses with their riders. She reached up, as if it was a giant balloon that she might be able to catch, but its seeming closeness was illusory. Fearful that she might lose sight of it, she climbed up a tree and watched it wistfully as it receded slowly over the tree-tops. It left a trail through the fog which did not close up. Far away, it illuminated the walls and roofs of the city.

Now she knew where the city was, she hurried through the trees, pushing aside bushes and branches in her haste. Badrur had not been at the school, and her sense of disappointment, of being cheated, still burned sulkily within her. If he was anywhere, he would be where that golden ball of light was – in the city. And this time she would find him.

In the Square, the two opposing forces faced each other. On one side were the remains of the city's inhabitants, among them Tancred, Astar, Herbie and

Jessie, and their moonhorses. On the other side were the moonghosts, more visible now than they had ever been, ugly, agitated, menacing, yet flickering with fear too. In the centre, between the two giant horses, the ball of fire, where the two beams of light met and clashed, flared more fiercely than ever.

Cassie clasped her brother tightly: in essence they were one. They felt rooted in the Diamond Horse, as if they were all part of one flesh. The bluish light that streamed from the diamond coursed through them too. They were hardly conscious of being human any more – it felt as if they were no more than a vessel for a powerful source of energy.

Prince Badrur was at one with the Horse of the Eclipse too. Currents of the night swirled through him, hatred flared like lightning. His mounting frustration at not being able to break the deadlock was like a series of implosions within him, sucking him into ever darker black holes of fury.

No surrender was possible for either. This could go on for an age, outside time, or so it seemed.

The fog was thinner in the city, and the Child blundered through its deserted streets towards a faint glow of light ahead. She sensed the pull of something within her, drawing her forward; and as she drew near the Square, she gave little shrieks and cries and laughs of anticipation. Badrur was the one fixed point in her dark heart, and she knew she was near him.

The crowd in the Square did not scatter in panic when they saw her: weakened by their coughs, profoundly moved by the cosmic battle being enacted before them between the two horses, the sight of the giant Child seemed just another part of the nightmarish scene unfolding before them.

Her eyes were drawn to the ball of crackling fire hovering midway between the two horses; it so dazzled and delighted her, she looked at nothing else. She ran across the Square, hands outstretched towards it. Moonghosts shrank back. Badrur turned and shuddered in horror. The twins felt a surge of hope.

The Child reached out with both hands for the ball of light. She touched it. There was a terrific flash. She screamed and fell back.

She looked at her throbbing hands in astonishment. The pain flared, and she cried, long, wrenching sobs, as she shook her hands to try and rid them of the pain. To everyone then – except for Badrur – she looked at that moment to be no more than an oversized infant that had been hurt. The instinct was to comfort her; but of course everyone held back.

Badrur laughed: serves her right, he thought. "Go. Shoo!" he shouted at her, waving his hand dismissively. "Go on, get out of here. No one wants you here."

She barely heard him through her pain.

Cassie stared at her more intently than anyone. She had helped bring this Child into the world; she had always felt responsible for her. That had been like a reproach; now, the healer in her came forward, and she wanted to comfort. On impulse, she slid off the back of the Diamond Horse. Keiron, left alone, half-heartedly protested, and the Horse neighed, feeling a sudden loss of power.

She approached the Child cautiously. How large, how frightening the Child looked, dirty and ragged, red-faced and tear-streaked from crying, writhing about on the ground in pain. Yet, how pitiful too.

Cassie came as near as she dared. The Child looked at her. Cassie tried to avoid looking into her eyes, remembering how dark and fathomless they had been when she had first looked into them, recalling how she felt they might suck her in and leave her floating like a dead thing in space.

"Give me your hands," she said.

The Child stopped whimpering and held out her burnt fingers. Cassie took a deep breath, took one more step forward and laid her hands over the Child's fingers. They were large and inflamed. She closed her eyes and willed her healing powers to flow outward. It was difficult, far more difficult than she had ever experienced before. The flow was checked by darkness, by deadness, and she had to fight through that as through a thick fog. Cassie had to concentrate everything she had inside her to make the breakthrough. *And it wasn't enough.*

The Child began to whimper again, to flex her throbbing fingers. Another few seconds and...

Suddenly, Cassie felt something tapping her foot. Will! He was holding Keiron's spur pendant. *Put it on her hand,* he mimed several times, and she understood. She snatched it from him and almost threw it over the Child's right hand just as it was withdrawing. Will pointed to his neck, and she understood that too. She pulled her own spur pendant off and threw that over the Child's left hand.

The Child stopped whimpering and looked at the two little golden necklaces dangling from her fingers. Cassie feared she might take them off, but after she had held them up to admire them, she wriggled them down on to her wrists. Through her tears, she gave Cassie a wan and thankful smile.

"Oh, give me strength," Badrur suddenly jeered. He had watched this little scene, fascinated like everyone else, but now he was fearful that Cassie was getting the Child on her side.

Cassie glanced at him but said nothing. She stepped forward and seized the Child's fingers again. Now the healing power flowed out of her with ease. She saw the flesh regenerate, the burnt skin heal over, she felt the pain fade out. In a few minutes the Child's hands were healed.

The Child sprang to her feet.

Cassie's heart was in her mouth. She thought she was about to be crushed in the Child's grateful hug. But the Child, just in time, saw her fear, and checked herself. They were so close now, Cassie could not avoid looking up into her eyes. She saw great dark spaces there, but there were stars in them now, and she no longer felt she was being sucked into them.

The Child sensed the difference too and became very quiet. "Cassie," she said, remembering. "Cassie." She held up her wrists as if to say thank you for her gift.

"Keep them," Cassie said, hoping she would understand. She knew their power would bring a little light into the creature's veiled existence – it was already happening.

The Horse of the Eclipse hit a hoof impatiently on the Square, causing sparks to fly. Badrur, sensing things were not going his way, urged his steed to a final, supreme effort, to catch the Diamond Horse at a weak moment. Cassie turned and saw Keiron beckoning urgently to her. She could see the Diamond Horse was straining against the dark beam that poured in ever greater strength from the Horse of the Eclipse, and the burning ball was edging nearer and nearer towards him.

What should she do? To return to Keiron was to return to deadlock.

Will stabbed at her ankle again with his sharp little wooden finger. She looked down, saw him make a gesture, and she understood. What a wise little manikin he was.

The Child was watching her in gratitude. She recalled their brief encounter in the school; but vaguer memories of this girl were flooding back too, now that the pain had gone. She remembered her at the battle with the monsters. She remembered her at the Sacred Spring telling her to unblock the waters. And, in the deeper past, she remembered something, a gasp of air, a pulse of light, somehow linked to her eyes.

Cassie, glancing at her again, took all this in. She summoned all the courage she had. Tentatively, she took hold of the Child's hand, grasping no more than one of the large fingers, and slowly led the Child towards Badrur and the Horse of the Eclipse. Here she was, sandwiched between one kind of evil and another, and she was acutely aware of how vulnerable she was.

Badrur tried to slash at her with a sword he'd appropriated from one of the guards, but she kept just out of his reach. The Child growled at him. How dare he attack the girl who had taken away her pain!

Cassie pointed to the Spur on Badrur's left ankle, and said to the Child, "Spur. Spur. Go and get his Spur." At first she did not understand, and Cassie had to point to the spur pendants on the Child's wrists, and then to her ankle, saying its name.

Delighted to be able to do something for this kind girl, the Child lunged suddenly towards the Horse of the Eclipse and the Rider. The Horse reared up in fright. Badrur clung on, trying at the same time to slash with his sword. It had no effect on the Child. She seized his leg and pulled him from his mount. As he sprawled and wriggled indignantly on the ground, she tore off the left Golden Spur.

She returned to Cassie, who had edged back, and held out the Spur to her.

"Take it," she heard her father say close by. "I think you've earned it, don't you."

Cassie took the Golden Spur from a solemn-looking Child. It shone like a jewel in her hand. She smiled at the Child, then held up the Spur so that everyone could see it.

Badrur, now on his feet, sprang forward desperately to snatch it from her, but Tancred was ready for him. He seized Badrur's arm, twisted it up behind his back, so that the prince cried out in fury and pain, and then he propelled Badrur straight into the arms of the Child.

The Child hugged him, almost squeezing him to death. At last she had got hold of him.

"Take him away," Cassie said to her. "Far away," and she waved with her hand to make herself clear. The Child understood. Tossing the bellowing, protesting Badrur over her shoulder, she ambled off across the Square, laughing to herself. She paused once to look back, suddenly wistful, at the girl; and then the fog beyond the Square began to swallow her up.

There was a muted and relieved cheer from the crowd.

"Cassie," Keiron was shouting. "You must get back on the Diamond Horse."

The ball of fire had moved back towards the Horse of the Eclipse now, and the black steed was struggling, but still full of formidable power. Keiron sensed a sudden determination in the Diamond Horse to eliminate his supreme enemy, his haunting and destructive shadow. With both Golden Spurs on his dual rider, he had the means at last to do it. The moment he had been waiting for, patiently preparing for, all these centuries, was upon them. The Horse of the Eclipse, aware that the supreme moment was upon him too, struggled violently to break from the beam of light and shadow that held him and his adversary, and Keiron feared he might succeed.

Lord Tancred knelt down and fixed the right Golden Spur to his daughter's ankle. "Now, get back on the Diamond Horse," he said, "and annihilate the Horse of the Eclipse for ever."

She leapt back up on to the Diamond Horse and felt Keiron's arms fold round her. The Diamond Horse neighed once, softly. A golden pool of light radiated out from them. Suddenly, the twins felt invincible. Fear and tension drained away. They watched without feeling now as the Horse of the Eclipse writhed in despair.

The Diamond Horse's beam of light bore the ball of fire relentlessly towards the Horse of the Eclipse. Closer and closer. There was no escape. The ball of fire reached the Horse of the Eclipse. He shrieked in pain, in anger, in fear.

And then, in a great flash, the Horse of the Eclipse was engulfed in flames. He twisted and shrieked, a dark shadow in the conflagration. No one felt sorry for him, for all knew, the pressing crowd, the twins, Astar, Jessie, Herbie, the Councillors and Tancred, that this was the only way.

Like torches all around the fire, the moonghosts that had guarded and watched him burst into flames too, and within seconds, as if there was no substance to burn, they flared up and died down, leaving a twist of smoke and a fragment of ash where once they had hovered.

Implacably, the twins watched the horse's final destruction. They did not feel exultation or relief, or anything but a sense that they were the channel for an inevitable force. But as the last of the of the horse's wings shrivelled up, as the dark outline in the fire crumbled, and the flames folded in on themselves, the image of his destruction was burnt into their hearts and would live with them for ever, not as a nightmare, but as a beacon in dark times ahead.

On the ground where the Horse of the Eclipse once stood was burnt a dark outline, like a permanent shadow; a few white ashes glowed, and the breeze scattered them across the Square.

* * *

With the moonghosts destroyed, the people suddenly felt wholesome and cured: the transformation from pain and darkness to light and health was so miraculous, they lost control of themselves for a while; they danced, laughed, cried, hugged, even burst into song.

The twins watched them contentedly, feeling happy and tired. They slipped off the Diamond Horse and quietly stroked him. His light flashed over them and his blue eyes glimmered with deep happiness.

"We – I mean, you – have united the Golden Spurs after, oh, I don't know how many years," their father said, about to launch into one of his well-meant but slightly pompous speeches. He was interrupted by the sudden appearance of Numero. The boy had heard his last words, and he said with a grin, "One thousand, seven hundred and twenty-eight years to be precise."

"Numero!" Cassie cried, delighted to see him again. "Where did you spring from?"

"Just arrived. My moonhorse – all the moonhorses, I gather – got a message from the Diamond Horse to meet here. You did fantastically, Cassie. Both of you did. Oh, to see the Horse of the Eclipse being devoured by those flames! It was wonderful!"

"You look so well, Numero," Keiron observed, smiling at his enthusiasm.

"Only for the last few minutes! As soon as the moonghosts turned into flames, I felt the last of my sickness burn up inside me. I feel fantastic. But I must join the others."

He pointed across the Square to where the moon-horses were gathering.

The twins watched, a little puzzled, as the eleven other Riders mounted their moonhorses and spread out in a circle, moving the crowd back to the edge of the Square as they did so. Numero ran eagerly to join them.

"Come on," Jessie called to them. "Join the circle."

The twins, still wearing the Golden Spurs, remounted the Diamond Horse. Slowly, they progressed around the circle. The Horse stopped at each moonhorse, and beamed light from the diamond into the creature's moonstone. Then he took his place and completed the circle.

Together, the twelve moonhorses flapped their wings, slowly, in unison, like a dance. A sphere of soft golden light, like sunshine, formed around them, and as they continued to flap their wings, the light widened and widened, taking in the Square and its people, the statues, the Sanctuary building; then it spread out into the city. The fog shrank before it. The light transformed the city, from the grey and fog-bound, the dank and dismal, to a place of light and creeping life, of sudden warmth. People who had been in hiding, or too sick to move, emerged pale, blinking, bemused and happy. The city was like a prisoner, incarcerated in some deep dungeon for countless years, being released at last into sunshine.

The light rippled out beyond the city, into the Eleven Estates, where the animals lifted their heads and sniffed the air disbelievingly, where the birds sang ecstatically in the blue of the sky, where Estate workers and Councillors met in the gardens and marvelled at the sunshine on their heads. It even penetrated the shadows of the vast forest, seeped through the canopies of dark, tough leaves and into the ground where seeds had lain dormant for centuries.

It made the Child in the forest drop Badrur, bruised all over and gasping for breath, unceremoniously on the ground, and twirl around the trees, trying to find the best patch of sunshine. Badrur saw his opportunity and fled, crashing through the trees in panic. He was lucky to stumble on a shingle track, and there he stood, against a tree, taking great lungfuls of breath, listening for any signs of the Child.

He had escaped.

But he saw in the patch of blue sky glimmering through the leaves the defeat of all his ambitions here, and he curled his lip in disgust. Well, he would make for the coast and find a ship. There was still the Golden Sword on South Island. He'd have that, if nothing else. And this time he would win.

Late that evening the twins, their father, the Ancient Riders, Torke, Marsia, Helyna and several other Councillors, held an impromptu party. Food and drink were brought by grateful townspeople, and rather boring speeches of thanks were made, some of which made the twins blush with embarrassment.

Now the sun was setting and the people had gone home to make their own family celebrations.

The Diamond Horse, who had stood quietly in the middle of the Square, on the mosaic of the Spurs, allowing himself to be admired but not touched by the people, flapped his great wings and looked intently at the twins. They all gathered around the great creature.

"If only he could talk," Keiron said.

"Well," said Marsia, "isn't it obvious what he wants?"

Cassie laughed and clapped her hands. "To ride with us, of course, Keiron! Think how long he's been waiting for that."

The Diamond Horse neighed softly in agreement.

"Go on, then," said their father. "Ride him for as long as you like. All night, if you want to."

"Can we?" Keiron exclaimed, his eyes glowing; and then he dashed towards the great beast, took a flying leap and landed on the Diamond Horse's back. "Come on, Cassie," he shouted.

He helped her mount. They each wore a Golden Spur.

"I shall be at Councillor Torke's town house," their father said, smiling proudly. "I'll see you there. Take as long as you like. But don't forget to return with the Spurs. Citatha is waiting for them."

The twins rose, leaving their father and friends far below, and the whole island stretched out around them, clear and sunlit. They could even see the sea glinting far away. The Diamond Horse flew to the coast and followed it right round the island, as if ringing it with the light from his diamond.

It was night when they landed in the Mooncastle. Here, the Diamond Horse could pass through walls, just as they had done. They settled in the room with the carvings of the twelve horses and their Ancient

Riders. Miraculously, food and drink appeared on the table: moonapples glowing softly green, and translucent blue pears, goblets with a milky liquid, and strange, moon-shaped sweets. The twins feasted. They offered food to the Diamond Horse, but he shook his head.

He settled down on the floor. They sat leaning against him, and when sleep stole over them, he folded his wing over them.

They spent three enchanted days in the Mooncastle. Time had no substance here.

But on the third day, the Diamond Horse, whose gestures and neighs they had grown to understand, insisted on their mounting him. The roof of the Mooncastle opened up and he flew out, up above the glassy turrets and away towards the city.

Saying goodbye to him, when they reached the city, was painful. It was like something essential being torn from their hearts.

A long procession wound its way behind the twins and their father south of the city, taking in the extremity of each of the Estates. It swelled to include all the Ancient Riders and their moonhorses, their families, city people out for a jaunt, Estate workers and servants eager for a holiday. Torke and Marsia entertained everyone with stories at night in the great Estate houses, and there were numerous banquets.

The endless sunshine had a tonic effect on the island's inhabitants. To them a blue sky, an occasional white cloud, and above all the blazing sun, were a miracle. It transformed their world and gave them all a new life. What greater excuse did they need to celebrate and be merry?

They came at last to the harbour where the ship was still moored. It had been kept in good repair by the crew, ready for sail.

The twins said goodbye to the moonhorses for the last time. The Ancient Riders crowded around them, pressing little gifts and mementoes into their hands, whispering last jokes and farewells, hugging or shaking hands. It was difficult and emotional for the twins, for on this island they had found for the first time a group of peers to whom they belonged. But they had cried themselves dry saying farewell to the Diamond Horse, and all they could do now was smile and hug and promise to return one day.

They boarded the ship.

"Goodbye, Astar," Cassie cried across the water. "I shall never forget our friendship."

"See you, Jessie," Keiron shouted

"When you get fed up with Will," Jessie shouted back. "Send him to me."

Not a bad idea, said Will with a laugh.

I shall remember that, Keiron retorted.

"Come, hold up the Golden Spurs," Lord Tancred gently urged, having stood aside patiently while his children had made their prolonged farewells. At times like this he felt sorry for his children, sorry that they should be wrenched away from their new friends, not being able to put down roots, always journeying.

The twins held up the Spurs which had been until then hanging around their necks like pendants. They turned towards Temple Island across the sunlit water.

The tunnel of of golden light, wide as a highway, held no surprises for them now: it arched over the sea and enfolded the ship. The vessel rose serenely into the tunnel and began its calm voyage back to Temple Island.

"I had my doubts we'd ever find the Spurs, I must admit," said Tancred. "But somehow you two have an uncanny knack of knowing where to look. You've found the Helmet, the Shield and now the Spurs, for the goddess. She knew what she was doing when she picked you two!"

"I wonder why she did, though?" Cassie mused.

They drifted on in silence through the golden tunnel.

Keiron sighed. He suddenly felt rather homesick. If he couldn't stay with his friends on West Island, he'd rather be going home to North Island, to a world that was his own, familiar.

You'd soon get bored, said Will.

Me? All I've ever wanted is a good storybook!

Cassie said nothing.

"What are you thinking about, Cass?" Keiron asked her eventually.

"The Child."

"Don't fret yourself about her. She'll be all right. And she'll have a nice time tormenting Badrur."

"It's not that. I was thinking that each time Badrur has got us just where he wants us, she comes along and saves us. She doesn't do it on purpose, but. . ."

Keiron saw her drift. "So," he said softly, "bringing her into this world without a soul wasn't such a dreadful thing, after all, was it? That's what you're thinking."

She nodded. "And there was something else. She's changed a bit, I think."

"She's growing up. Fast!"

"No, more than that. Something I saw in her eyes. Not just darkness, emptiness, death. Stars, light, glimmers of life."

"The pendants will help her, I'm sure."

"Yes, that was a good idea of yours."

"There's hope for her yet."

"Maybe," said Cassie, nodding thoughtfully. Bringing the Child into life without a soul had been like a dark persistent shadow inside her; now for the first time, she felt that shadow begin to lift.

The vault beneath the ruined temple on Temple Island was very quiet. The stillness was almost palpable. The Helmet, staring at the ceiling, seemed on the point of speaking, and the Shield, which suddenly brought to mind their friend Justus the lizard-boy, glowed softly, honey-coloured in the dim light. The suit of Golden Armour, giving off a pale light, seemed somehow almost alive, as if it had just laid down to sleep.

The twins clipped the Spurs on to the Armour. The light around it intensified, and they stood back.

"Only the Sword now," came the goddess's voice. They looked about them, and felt her to be close, but she did not reveal herself. "North Island is beautiful now," she breathed, in her strange, disembodied voice. "East Island is springing with new life. I have been to both since you helped to transform them. Now I shall go to West Island. Three-quarters of my former world is like the paradise it was. And the greatest is yet to come."

A silver cat appeared in the doorway and mewed gently. Cassie gathered it into her arms, and Keiron stroked it. The cat's purr made them all feel happy, and in the tranquil days they spent resting on the little island, it never left their side.

"It'll soon be time to leave for South Island," Tancred said one morning, his brow creasing, his white beard stirring in the breeze.

Will shuddered.

Why did you do that? Keiron asked.

The minute he said South Island, I saw a hideous sea-monster. Now I see a stone giant imprisoned in a mountain, and a wild girl leaping through the trees. A world full of reflections... His voice in Keiron's head trailed away. Ah, well, there would be time enough for that, Will thought; and as the cat was passing at that moment, he jumped on her back and rode away before Keiron could ask any more.

Have you read the
first book in the series?

GOLDEN
ARMOUR

THE HELMET

Tara the wolf-girl stood in the shelter of an oak tree and shivered. The cold wind buffeted the tree-tops and crept icily through the undergrowth. In the forest clearing, the wolf-people had arrived back home, having served for a month as servants in the Mansion. They were milling about excitedly, yapping, licking, nipping, barking, rolling about in the leaves together. Tara watched them, sad and yearning.

Mingling with the welcomes were loud and tearful farewells. Those who were going back to the Mansion, as replacement servants, slipped regretfully out of their skins, and stood naked and shivering as humans in the frosty moonlight. The new arrivals seized their discarded skins and wriggled into them, a look of profound relief on their wolfish faces.

Tara had heard many stories of the Mansion, of the ways of humans, of their peculiar smell and lack of fur, of their cunning and mastery. One of the humans was now visible above the commotion. Aulic. He was standing on a sledge, wrapped in a great black bearskin, waving his arms about, shouting.

She watched restlessly, softly yapping to herself. Circling the edge of the clearing, and averting her eyes from the scenes of reunion, she paused behind a log and watched Aulic. How ugly he was, how powerful; he struck an obscure terror in her. But humans fascinated her. She had watched them hunting and trapping: they seemed so slow and helpless on their two legs, and yet so dangerous.

Stepping from behind the log, she paused at the edge of the clearing, wondering what she should do. Naked wolf-people were clambering on to the carts and sledges, huddling together under deer- and bear-skins.

She had been told of the children of the Mansion, of Keiron and Cassie: two exalted human children with no mother and an eccentric father. She had heard how Cassie had often been there to welcome the new batch of wolf-servants, to warm them with kind words and see that they were settled in; and of how Keiron would show them through all the dark and twisting passages of the great house.

Aulic gracelessly accepted a horn of water from a wolf-woman, and gulped down the cold, brackish liquid. He flung the horn aside, swore at any wolf-person in sight and shouted at the more timid stragglers: "Get a move on. I'm not waiting any longer."

For some time now, Tara had had an obscure sense that she stood apart from her pack. Was she the only one who was reluctant to return to her wolf-skin? Who sometimes found her human form more beautiful than her wolf one? Often, she yearned to strike out into the dark forest on her own. But where would she go?

As she watched the wolf-people huddling under the furs on the giant sledges, ready to set out for the Mansion, an impulse rose up in her, a crackle of energy that made her leap up and yelp. She was much too young to serve in the Mansion, but that wasn't going to stop her now. She raced over the clearing towards the nearest sledge, even as Aulic was signalling for them to leave.

Tara heard voices behind her, calling her back, but she did not heed them. With one concentrated twist of her body, she shed her skin. She felt a pang of remorse as it slid to her feet, but she knew that it would be well looked after in her absence. Not pausing to look at her moon-white human form, she clambered on to the nearest sledge and slid under a pile of furs.

"It's not your turn, girl," voices among the furs said. "You're too young." But it was too late, whips were being cracked, horses were snorting, sledges were turning: they were on the move.

An hour later, they emerged from the wind-torn forest and struck out over rugged brush. Here the full force of the wind hit them, threatening to snatch away their mounds of furs. The horses struggled on, their heads bent, goaded by the sting of whips. Tara felt the cold envelop her; she pulled the dead skins tighter around her, realizing the mad sacrifice she had made in leaving her own skin behind.

At last they came to the top of a high, flat ridge, where the horses were allowed to catch their breath. Far away in the distance a cold, metallic sea glittered fitfully in the moonlight between scudding clouds. Below them, on the rocky coast, stood the Mansion, a sprawling, shadowy building, surrounded by outbuildings and a circling wall. Faint lights flickered in many windows.

They trotted the last stretch down to the house, the horses breathing heavily after their long trek.

The great gates of the Mansion opened to swallow them up. The wolf-people emerged from their sledges, blinking and apprehensive, jostling together uncertainly in a dank courtyard. No stories of the Mansion ever prepared them for the first shock of that dark and gloomy place of shadows.

Tara was in panic at being hemmed in and surrounded by looming walls and turrets. She hid behind a rotting water-butt against a wall. She heard Aulic telling them to enter the Mansion at once. She wanted to join them, but she felt paralysed with a nameless fear. She curled her strange, elongated body into a tight ball, wishing for her wolf-tail that it might cover her eyes.

After what seemed an endless time, she felt a warm hand on her arm and heard a soft, coaxing voice. She shrank back and opened her eyes.